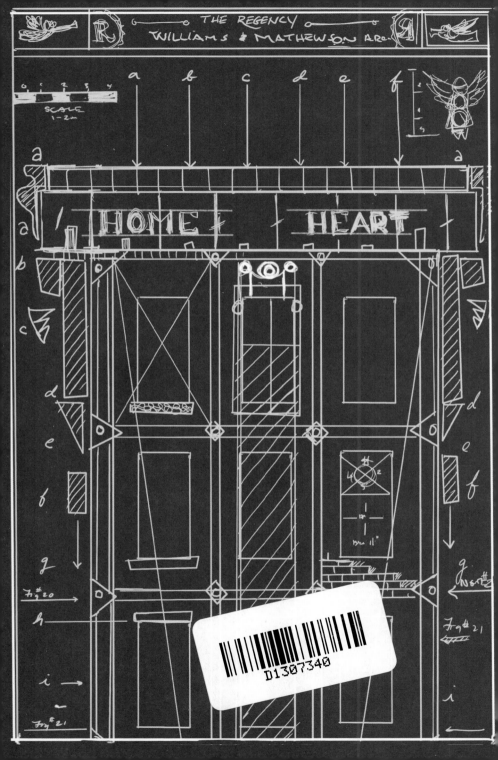

APARTMENT 713

ALSO BY KEVIN SYLVESTER

NOVELS
The Fabulous Zed Watson! (with Basil Sylvester)
The MINRs Trilogy
The Neil Flambé Capers
The Hockey Super Six series
The Almost Epic Squad: Mucus Mayhem

PICTURE BOOKS
Gargantua Jr: Defender of Earth
Super-Duper Monster Viewer
Splinters

ILLUSTRATED BY KEVIN
Great Too
Great

NON-FICTION
Follow Your Stuff (with Michael Hlinka)
Follow Your Money (with Michael Hlinka)
Basketballogy
Baseballogy
Game Day
Showtime
Gold Medal for Weird
Sports Hall of Weird

ILLUSTRATED BY KEVIN
Don't Touch that Toad

APARTMENT
713

➤ A Novel ⇐

KEVIN SYLVESTER

HarperCollins*PublishersLtd*

Published by HarperCollins Publishers Ltd

First edition

HarperCollins books may be purchased for educational, business,
or sales promotional use through our Special Markets Department.

HarperCollins Publishers Ltd
Bay Adelaide Centre, East Tower
22 Adelaide Street West, 41st Floor
Toronto, Ontario, Canada
M5H 4E3

www.harpercollins.ca

Library and Archives Canada Cataloguing in Publication

Title: Apartment 713 / Kevin Sylvester. | Names: Sylvester, Kevin, author.
Identifiers: Canadiana (print) 20220257353 | Canadiana (ebook) 2022025737x
ISBN 9781443460941 (hardcover) | ISBN 9781443460958 (ebook)
Classification: LCC PS8637.Y42 A73 2022 | DDC jC813/.6—dc23

Printed and bound in the United States

24 25 26 27 28 LBC 7 6 5 4 3

To Jack Kelly,
who took us on the most amazing architectural walks . . .
and is a great host

Reader's Dedication
I dedicate this to

_____

(Who helped make you the reader you are today?)

APARTMENT 713

CHAPTER ONE

Jake Simmons slumped on the end of his bed and stared at the peeling wallpaper. The pattern might once have been a grapevine or flowers, but now it was so faded he couldn't tell. Flakes of yellowed plaster clung to the back.

A slight breeze rustled the scrap, tearing a few more crumbs of plaster away from the wall. Jake turned.

The window was closed.

"Great," Jake said. "This dump is either haunted or busted."

The glass rattled in the frame as the wind whipped up again.

"What's that, Jake?" came his mother's voice from the next room.

"I said, 'This place sucks.'"

There was a loud sigh, the rustling of paper, shifting of boxes, but no other reply.

Jake began picking at the wallpaper. More plaster came away from the wall, flakes falling like snow onto the stained grey rug and scuffed planks of the wooden floor.

"THIS. PLACE. SUCKS!" he yelled.

With an angry lurch, he ripped an entire strip from the wall. The uneven gash stared back like a snarling mouth. The exposed plaster was cracked and in parts even missing, revealing dusty wooden slats underneath.

"Stop that, please." His mother's annoyed voice, this time from the doorway.

Jake stared at the strip of paper, so fragile it would crack into pieces if he pinched. He pinched.

"I miss our old place."

"I know," she said quietly, leaning on the doorjamb.

"I miss my room. My games. I miss having a window that doesn't breathe."

The glass rattled. He swore.

"Language."

"Why? Because our neighbours can hear us through these stupid paper-thin walls?" He slapped on the wooden slats, sending a puff of dust into the air and onto the rug.

"I know." His mother's head dipped lower.

"Why did we have to move to this dump?"

His mom took a deep breath. They'd been over this a hundred times. "You know why. We had no choice. My job. Then when Janice left, I couldn't . . ." An even deeper sigh. "It was this or . . ."

"Whatever." He let the scrap of wallpaper drop to the floor.

"Look, Jake. It's a place to stay. For now. Until we can find something better. Until we can get back on our feet, you know?"

"I don't know how you get back on your feet when they stick to the kitchen floor."

His mom ran her fingers through her hair and pursed her lips. "My grandpa left me this place when he died."

"Great-Grandpa?" This was new info. "Did he lose a bet or something?"

His mom ignored that. "It was kind of a family mystery. There was this key on his mantel when we were kids." She stopped for a moment, remembering.

Jake listened, trying as hard as he could to look like he wasn't.

"Grandpa said it was a key for something called the Regency. It sounded so grand, but he never told us what it actually was. He said the Regency had been there for him, though, and would be here for us if we had no other choice."

"Can't imagine any other reason to stay here," Jake mumbled. *Some mystery*, he thought.

"Fine." His mom closed her eyes and turned to leave. Then she stopped, fists clenched, and spoke without looking back. "It's all I . . . we . . . have left. And maybe, if you stop ripping the paper off the walls, we can make it a *home*."

She marched away toward a wall of cardboard boxes.

Jake sat perfectly still for a good half hour while his mother worked away in the outer rooms. He stared at the stains on the rug, the flakes of crumbled paper, the dust from the walls.

His old life had been awesome. When he'd looked out of his old window of his suburban house, he'd seen trees and a big green yard. A wide paved driveway led to a wide paved road.

Here? All he could see through the grimy window was the even grimier window of an even dumpier building.

His old bedroom walls had been covered with posters of his favourite bands, baseball players, video gamers.

His shoulders sagged. Gaming? That was gone. His video game setup was one of the things they'd sold to pay for the move.

3

There, he'd had high-speed internet and a first-class TV.

Here? No TV. An old laptop that his mom used. High-speed internet? Jake laughed.

His posters were rolled up in a cardboard tube. Apparently one of the stupid rules of this stupid building was that you couldn't put holes in the wall. No tacks. No nails.

He stared at the cracked plaster and torn wallpaper. And they're worried about NEW holes? He snorted.

What had his mom meant when she said, "Grandpa left me this place"? Who leaves an apartment to somebody? Great-Grandpa hadn't even lived here. He'd lived in a house in a totally different city. Had he owned this place? That meant Jake and his mom did now, right? And if they owned it, why couldn't they put HOLES. IN. THEIR. OWN. WALLS?

He was about to yell again, but a muffled sob from the other room stopped him short. It was a sound he'd heard a lot over the past few weeks. His mom had had what she called "a great job" as a legal secretary. That was gone. Her latest relationship? Over. Janice had been really nice, and fun too—while she'd stayed. She loved to talk about comic books and movies. But there had been arguments about money, and then about having no money, and then . . .

Jake missed her.

Another muffled sob. Jake stayed on his bed.

He'd hugged his mom plenty lately. He loved her. He really did. But now, being banished to this . . . this *place*, he just couldn't go out and hug her right now. Even thinking about it made his cheeks burn. He didn't even know why, and that made him angry at himself.

Did he blame her? Maybe.

4

Jake got up and closed his door as quietly as possible.

He shuffled back toward his bed, passing the unopened cardboard boxes of his stuff.

He opened the top flap of the nearest box, saw the T-shirt Janice had given him for his birthday, then closed it violently. He kicked the side so hard his foot broke through the cardboard.

He pulled his foot out, kicked the box again, then slumped on his bed, burying his head in his pillow.

CHAPTER TWO

Jake gently closed the door of the apartment, careful not to let his mom hear him leave. They'd been at the Regency for about a week. He hadn't left his bed, except to eat, shower, and go to the bathroom.

It wasn't curiosity that finally pushed him out of his apartment but a mix of boredom and frustration. He needed to get away from his mom. From the mess. His mom had unpacked and organized the other rooms. He'd done the occasional dive into his own boxes for clean underwear and socks, but that had left his room even messier. Putting away his things seemed to him like a sign this move was permanent.

He was in no mood for any of that. So he'd decided to explore.

The lock clicked shut. Jake held his breath, but no footsteps sounded from the other side of the door.

He stood up straight, exhaled slowly, and looked down the hallway. "Ugh," he said. "Regency? You *are* a dump."

The wallpaper was faded where it wasn't ripped or torn.

The red carpet was worn so thin you could see the floorboards peeking through from underneath.

Jake had read books about people who ended up in places like this. "Ended" being the key word.

He walked slowly away from his door.

He was careful to avoid the walls, worried he'd stain his last decent sweatshirt if he brushed against whatever grime covered the paper.

Jake didn't have a great idea of where to go. He'd barely noticed any details about the building the day they'd moved in, except that they were on the ninth—and top—floor. He'd helped unload the moving van that they could barely afford and had mostly focused on the tops of his shoes and the cracked pavement. He'd stared at the sidewalk like he wanted to bore a hole through it and escape.

Should he try to find a way to the roof? Maybe he could catch a glimpse of his old home. His shoulders sagged. The Regency, Jake thought, was in a different part of reality. He might as well have been looking for a house on Mars.

Jake was more of an inside kid anyway. And outside was raining cat and dogs, as Janice used to say.

Inside it only smells *like cats and dogs*, he thought with a wry chuckle.

The lights flickered as Jake made his way down the empty hallway. There were nine other apartments on his floor, and he leaned an ear against the door of each one but heard nothing.

"Hello? Anyone else here?" His voice echoed down the hallway. "Empty."

He looked around for an elevator, to see if—as he expected—the other floors were as depressing as his, but he couldn't find

one. They'd used the freight elevator, at the side of the building, to move in, but you needed a special key to operate that. It
had also smelled like someone puked inside. Or maybe died. Or
maybe both.

A painted sign at the end of the hallway read *Stairs*. Jake
walked over, took a breath, and pushed the door. It creaked
open.

The air in the stairwell was stale, like an old book that has
been left in a damp basement for decades. Jake gagged and
almost turned back, but then he heard his own door open and
his mom calling.

"Jake? Jake? Are you here? Can you help me with something? I have a call in five. Jake?"

The call his mom was going to make was for yet another
job she wasn't going to get. Jake hated the fake smile she put
on at the start of each one. But he hated even more the deflated
voice that said, "Sure. Thanks anyway," at the end. Sometimes
the other person had already hung up, so she didn't even get a
chance to say that.

He quietly closed the door behind him and tiptoed quickly
down the stairs.

Just as he passed the door to the fourth floor, he heard a
sound. He stopped. "Hello?"

"Meow," came softly back from under the door.

Jake carefully opened it a crack.

A tiny grey kitten poked its head through and brushed
against the toe of his sneaker. "Mew," it said.

"Hey, little guy." Jake stepped into the hallway and closed
the door to keep the kitten from escaping, then bent down to
stroke the soft fur. The kitten purred.

There was another meow as an orange cat began rubbing against his leg. Then another and another joined them.

"What the heck?" Jake looked down the hallway. A line of cats led to an open door. "Looks like you little guys made a jailbreak!"

He picked up the kitten and stepped carefully around the others. The door to apartment 405 was slightly ajar. Jake opened it and put the kitten down on the floor. It scuttered into the kitchen.

"Hello?" Jake called.

The kitten meowed from inside, and Jake heard something sliding over the tile floor.

He poked his head around the doorway.

An old woman was sitting at a small round table, staring into space. She was incredibly thin and wrapped in a faded robe, with a knitted shawl falling off one shoulder.

The kitten was under the table, pushing an empty bowl around with its paw. It looked at Jake, mewed, then wandered off into another room.

"Ma'am?" Jake said. "Is that your kitten?"

The woman turned toward him slowly. Her eyes were grey and slightly droopy, as if she was half asleep.

"Anastasia?" she said in almost a whisper.

"Um, my name is Jake. But if Anastasia is the kitten, I just dropped her off. The other cats followed us, so it's all good."

The woman gave an almost imperceptible nod, then went back to staring into space. After a moment, she began quietly singing a song Jake didn't know. She raised her right hand and waved it in the air in time with the tune.

The larger cats were surrounding her legs now, staring at the empty bowl, then up at her.

"Um, ma'am?" Jake said, taking a cautious step closer. "Are you okay? The cats seem like they might be hungry."

The woman continued singing. Then she shook with an unexpectedly powerful laugh.

Jake froze. But the woman stopped laughing just as abruptly, sat back in the chair, and continued her song. He wasn't sure whether to try to feed the cats or just turn and leave.

"Lily," said a deep voice from behind him, "how are you today?"

The woman's face broke into a huge grin. She stopped singing and turned, looking straight through Jake.

Jake turned too.

A huge man in a green shirt and pants was standing just inside the doorway, gently shooing a cat with the toe of his boot. A set of keys jangled from his belt.

"Steve, is that you?" Lily said.

"Sure is," said the man.

Jake looked at the name tag on the man's shirt, which clearly said "Danny."

The man winked at Jake and held a finger to his lips. "I'm just making sure Anastasia and the kids are all okay."

Lily seemed to notice the room—and the dozen or so cats milling around her legs—for the first time. But she didn't seem quite sure what to do about them. "Um, yes . . ." she said, then trailed off.

Danny, or Steve, put a hand on Jake's shoulder and gently moved him aside. "I know where the food is," he said, walking over to a cupboard by an ancient lime-green fridge.

"Yes, Steve. You were always such a nice boy," Lily said.

DannySteve pulled out a few cans of cat food. He opened one and plopped the contents into the bowl by Lily's feet.

She giggled as the cats rubbed against her ankles, jostling for position around the bowl.

"There's enough for everyone," the man said. He reached back into the cupboard and pulled out another half dozen or so tins and set them on the counter.

Jake started to walk backward toward the hallway, but Danny-Steve called him over and pointed at the cans. "If you could help me out a little bit here, son," he said, "it would be much appreciated."

Jake walked over to the counter and opened a can.

Lily now stared straight at Jake, her eyes narrowing for a moment.

"J . . . J?" she said, confused. Then the moment passed, and she giggled again as a satisfied cat leapt onto her lap and began purring.

DannySteve refilled the bowl, then patted Lily's hand and adjusted the shawl over her shoulder. Her skin was dotted with spots and looked like stretched dry paper. Jake could see the blue veins underneath.

DannySteve motioned for Jake to head out the door. "Lily, I'll be back later to check on you again, okay?"

"Steve!" Lily said. "I didn't know you were here!" Then she resumed petting the cat. DannySteve smiled at her.

Jake waited in the hallway, not sure what to do, as the man closed the door with a click behind them. Was he going to get yelled at for walking into a stranger's apartment?

"So is it Steve or Danny?" Jake asked quickly, trying to head off any reprimand.

"Danny. I'm the super here at the Regency." He held out an enormous hand.

Jake hesitated a moment, imagining his own fingers being crushed in a death grip. But the superintendent's handshake was surprisingly gentle.

"Jake."

"Welcome to the Regency, Jake. I met your mom when you were moving in. Tried to say hello to you, but you were a little preoccupied with your shoelaces." He chuckled.

"So what's wrong with . . ." Jake nodded toward the closed door to apartment 405.

"Lily? Nothing's wrong, per se. Just a little confused. She thinks I'm her grandson Steve. He and his family don't come around that often." He turned to look at her door and sighed. "But she's still an incredible sweetie. I think she's as old as this place."

"And *slightly* less decrepit," Jake joked.

Danny rolled his eyes. "Anyway, Jake, I'm just doing my afternoon rounds. Want to come for a tour?"

Jake took in the dumpy surroundings, and every cell in his body wanted him to say no. But his mom was probably still calling and calling and smiling and crying . . . so he just shrugged and said, "Sure."

CHAPTER THREE

T he doors to apartment 403 slid apart, revealing an iron grate and three ornate mirrored walls. Slightly scuffed marble tiles covered the floor. Apartment 403 didn't exist.

"There's a hidden elevator?" Jake's eyes grew wide.

Danny smiled. "It's one of many mysteries here at the Regency."

"Like how the building stays standing?" Jake chuckled.

Danny cocked his head. "Now, now. Be kind. This old beauty is filled with amazing things. Why is the elevator disguised as an apartment? No one knows."

Jake and Danny stepped inside. Unlike the hallways, the elevator seemed shiny and clean. The mirrors were framed in a deeply polished and intricately carved oak. Grapevines and leaves overlapped in a twisting, flowing pattern.

The panel for the buttons was a sheet of polished brass, each button sitting in its own circle, shining like a pearl. The number for each floor was etched into the button and inlaid with gold.

The button for the third floor seemed to be cracked down the middle. As far as Jake could tell, it was the only damage in the whole elevator. It was like they'd stepped into a different, much nicer building.

"Maybe whoever designed it to be hidden didn't want some random loser walking into the lobby and having access to the higher floors?" Jake said, running a finger along a vine.

"Maybe," Danny said. "But random losers, as you call them, aren't always what they appear to be."

"Meaning what?"

Danny didn't answer. "Have you read the inscription outside?"

"In-*what*?"

"Inscription. It runs outside, along the top of the Regency. Carved in the stone."

Jake shook his head.

Danny ran a finger through the air, as if he were tracing a line around the elevator ceiling. "It reads 'A home is a place with heart. A heart makes a place a home. This is my home. You are always welcome here.' Isn't that lovely?"

Jake shrugged, not exactly sure what Danny's point was. "Can you still read it? The outside bits I did see were pretty gross."

"That is true, I guess." Danny pushed a brass button with a *B* engraved on it. "But even a century of smoke, grime, and pigeon poop can't cover its beauty."

Jake couldn't agree less, but he decided, this time, to stay quiet.

The doors closed, along with an iron grate. It scraped against the opening, making a high-pitched squeal.

"It's a safety barrier," Danny said. "To stop people from leaning against the doors."

"Didn't keep my ears safe," Jake said.

"Yeah, I'll have to oil it again soon." Danny locked it in place.

There was a slight lurch, and the elevator began to go down.

Jake caught a glimpse of his reflection in the mirrors. Jakes spread away in a bendy line, getting smaller and smaller and smaller. He winked, and they all winked back. He made a silly face, and they made the same face back. He squinted to see the farthest version of himself, but Jakes seemed to go on forever.

The elevator stopped with another lurch. Danny undid the latch on the iron grate and the doors slid open, revealing—

"This the basement or the scrap heap?" Jake snarked.

Piles of metal machinery, pipes, cogs, and bolts sat on every available surface, including the floor. Jake wasn't completely sure what any of them were exactly, but he could tell they were metal, old, and rusted.

Danny walked past him, shaking his head. "Kids today."

Jake looked up. The ceiling was covered with twisting pipes, some thickly duct-taped at the joints, puffs of steam still escaping from the looser seals. Dust-covered wires spread from girder to girder in an ornate web, twirling around the piping and each other.

He looked back at the elegant vines that framed the elevator mirrors. This seemed like the upside-down version of that world.

Somewhere in the distance, a drop of water plinked.

"The Regency's intestines," Danny said with a laugh. "Not pretty, but necessary—like a human's guts—and mostly functional." He gently tapped the glass face on a brass dial attached

15

to a steel tank. The tank gave a rumble and then purred. "It's pretty much a full-time job keeping this all working."

"This is all working?!" Jake said, pretending to be shocked. A hiss of steam added an exclamation point to his joke.

"Ha-ha. Fine. Look, I know from the outside this building doesn't seem like much. Just one more old brick heap in a city with too many, right?"

Jake shrugged. "It's not so great from the inside either."

"But the Regency . . . it has more."

"More problems?"

Danny narrowed his eyes. "Clearly this tour isn't sinking in here." He tapped Jake's chest the same way he'd just tapped the dial.

Jake frowned. "I guess you started the tour at the literal bottom, so we should keep going up. Maybe it gets better."

"Just a second. I needed to stop here first to get a few things." Danny walked over to a giant wall of steel, curved like the side of a barrel.

"Is that a water boiler or something?"

Danny shook his head and grinned. He pushed one of the rivets, and a panel swung open, revealing a large circular room, the walls covered with oak.

One tiny window at the top let in a single beam of greyish sunlight.

"That's kinda cool," Jake said.

"One more mystery." Danny stepped inside.

The room had a desk with an antique telephone on top. Danny motioned to an old wooden office chair. The wood was gouged and worn, the green leather cushion split and cracked. Bits of foam stuffing leaked from the sides.

"Have a seat. I'll just be a second."

16

Jake sat down and instantly regretted it. The chair lurched to the left, and he had to reach out to steady himself. He was able to position the wheels to stabilize the chair, then slowly pulled himself toward the table. He picked up the phone handset. It felt like it weighed a hundred pounds. He put it to his ear. Nothing.

"Dead."

Jake wasn't surprised. He put it back in the cradle. Danny was pulling things in and out of slots on some old filing cabinet; above him, covering the wall, was a panel with rows of small red glass bubbles. Under each bubble was a brass plate with a number etched on it.

"What's that? Some kind of ancient pinball machine?" Jake said.

Danny looked up. "An alert system, actually. All of these lights are connected to different rooms. Didn't you notice the buzzer just inside your kitchen door?"

Jake had not.

"Well, if you need anything, you push that buzzer and it sends a message down here to this panel."

The light above plaque 804 lit up a bright red.

"For example, that's Gus wondering why I'm late."

"Gus?"

"Apartment 804. He gets a delivery every day."

"And *you* deliver it to him? Why can't he get it himself?"

Danny didn't answer. He picked up a package from his desk.

Jake looked back at the panel. The light for 713 was covered with layers of brittle electrical tape.

"Is that one broken?"

Danny looked at the panel for a few seconds. "There's nothing in there," he said. Then he added, "You can't go inside." He

17

shooed Jake out of the office and swung the door closed. "Let's just say that apartment 713 is off-limits."

He walked past Jake and into the elevator.

"Tour bus leaves in three, two—"

Jake jumped in just as the door began to close.

CHAPTER FOUR

The first stop wasn't Gus in 804. It was actually 415 and a woman whom Danny called the Professor. He walked into her apartment without even knocking and made his way straight to the kitchen.

Jake stood in the doorway and watched the woman in her living room, standing in front of a giant chalkboard. She was busily sketching and erasing a series of numbers, arrows, and symbols he didn't recognize. A laptop sat on a small table next to her, and she occasionally stopped to glance at something on the screen.

"Hello, ma'am," Jake called.

The woman didn't even flinch. She continued writing, erasing, looking, writing, erasing.

Friendly, Jake thought. "Well, bye! Nice chatting."

No response.

He shrugged and made his way into the kitchen. There was an off smell that got stronger as he got closer.

Danny was standing over the sink, tossing old fast food

containers into a garbage bag. Jake didn't need to see the rotting leftovers to know they were there.

"She gets a little dreamy when she's working on a project," Danny explained. "So I make sure her garbage doesn't get *too* bad."

"*Too* late," Jake said, waving his hand uselessly in front of his nose and trying not to throw up.

Danny tied up the full garbage bag and walked out of the apartment. Jake followed and closed the door behind him. When he turned, Danny was standing in front of the wall next to the elevator. He pushed the garbage bag into a hole in the wall. Jake did a double take when he noticed that the mouth of the chute was made to look like the head of a hippopotamus. Its tusked jaws actually opened and then closed as the bag slid away into the darkness.

"That's also kinda cool," Jake said.

Danny smiled. "Told you. This place has all sorts of surprises. C'mon, more deliveries to make."

They dropped off mail for Theo in 501. He was a piano player who didn't stop playing as Danny put down one stack of letters and picked up another. Theo's "music" sounded, to Jake's ears, like someone was torturing Lily's cats. He breathed a sigh of relief when Danny closed the door.

There was Irene, 602, who had left her keys in her mailbox. Again. Her apartment seemed to be filled with books and piles of loose paper. She looked like she hadn't had a proper haircut ever. Her sweater had holes she'd clearly tried and failed to fix herself.

Javier, 615, gave a shriek when Danny delivered a package from some company called When Wigs Fly.

The seventh floor seemed deserted, and Danny leaned

against a wall and checked his watch. He didn't even knock on any of the doors.

"Um, what are we waiting for? A ghost?" Jake asked. He'd started wondering way back on floor 5 why he was still on this weird little trip. But he lived on the ninth floor, and riding the golden elevator was better than stepping into that smelly stairwell again.

"Not a ghost," Danny said. "Just a friend."

"Uh-huh." Jake stole a peek at the door of 713. It seemed the same as all the others. He was about to walk up for a closer look when he heard a loud ding from the elevator. The doors to "703" opened, and a skinny guy in ripped shorts, ripped shirt, and ripped backpack bounded out. He had biking gloves and a helmet covered with skull stickers.

"Delaney." Danny nodded.

"Dude!" Delaney gave a wide smile. "Do you have it?"

Danny nodded again and handed Delaney a thick envelope.

Delaney actually gave a little jump and quickly tucked the envelope into a pocket in his backpack. Then he bear-hugged Danny, unlocked apartment 702, and bounded inside. The door closed with a loud click.

"What. The. Heck. Was that about?" Jake asked as Danny held open the elevator doors.

"I have a guy who knows a guy," Danny answered vaguely. "So I sometimes get Delaney some—"

"NOPE." Jake held up his hand. "Stop. I don't want to know."

Danny shrugged. "Okay. Suit yourself."

They got in the elevator.

"Is all this stuff really a super's job?" Jake asked as Danny closed the iron grate.

Danny gave a tiny smile. "At the Regency it is."

"No wonder you don't have time to fix all that stuff down-stairs."

"You wanna help out? I could use an assistant. Won't pay much, but—"

"Ha!" Jake snorted. "Not in a million years."

The elevator dinged and Danny opened the doors.

Gus—whoever he was—was the final stop.

Danny walked up to apartment 804 and gave a gentle rap on the door. He didn't wait for an answer but bent down and left the package on the floor. Then he stood up and turned around.

"Don't you want to make sure he's home?" Jake asked.

"He's always home." Danny stood in front of the elevator. "Thanks for keeping me company, Jake."

"Um, yeah." Jake kept his eyes locked on the package and the still-unopened door.

"I'm heading back down to the basement. You can find your way back to your apartment?"

Jake didn't answer. His mind was elsewhere. Back at his old house, his neighbour, Manic Miss Fredricks—Jake's nickname for her—had installed a camera on her door to stop thieves from taking her deliveries. It had happened one time, although Janice told Jake the package had just been delivered to the wrong house by the UPS guy. Still, Miss F. seemed to think that crooks were hiding in every hydrangea bush. Even Jake wasn't above suspicion. If he walked too close to her porch, she'd stare at him and point at the camera.

That Delaney guy from 702 seemed way sketchier than anyone from his old 'hood. Just the sort of guy who might run up to a porch or doorstep and grab an unprotected parcel.

Jake turned to look at Danny. "What if someone just walks by and steals it?"

Danny shook his head. "Gus will grab it as soon as he knows we're gone."

"What? Why?" Jake listened for any sign of life from the other side of the door but heard nothing.

He stared at the package. He wasn't even sure why he was suddenly so anxious. Something just made him want to be sure it was delivered safely. Out here, in the hallway, anything could happen. It was like coming across a newborn kitten—alone, abandoned, with no one to keep it safe, to protect it when things went wrong, when everything goes wrong . . .

He felt a lump in his throat, swallowed it hard, and marched up to Gus's door.

Danny stopped the elevator doors from closing.

"Jake, you need to leave or he won't come out."

Jake leaned against the door and spoke into the keyhole. "Gus, my name is Jake. You don't know me. I'm, uh, new here. I just moved in upstairs. Hi. I figure whatever is in this package is probably important to you, and I just . . . I dunno. I'm worried that if you don't grab it now, it might just . . . get lost." He stopped and put his ear to the door but still didn't hear anything.

Unexpected words popped into his head. "Gus, losing something precious or important is just . . . I'm tired of it. I'm fine to stay here and keep watch until you're ready. That's all. I'm stepping away from the door now."

Silence.

Silence.

Silence.

Then a shuffled footstep from inside and a click as someone unlocked the door.

A metal cane and then a heavily tattooed arm reached out to the package and slid it back into the room. Jake spied one tattoo of two eagles flying over a skull and crossed swords.

The sound of a radio came from deep inside the apartment. There was a loud crack and then cheering.

"You . . . you like baseball?" Jake asked.

The arm disappeared quickly, and the door closed with a click.

Silence again, broken by a low whistle from Danny in the doorway of the elevator.

Jake's brain was spinning. Why had he even cared about this weird stranger and his weird package? Why had he said what he said?

Then he thought of his mom, who'd lost almost everything. Who was upstairs right now, probably trying yet again to get a job when no one was hiring. Who had watched her life fall apart unexpectedly and was struggling to get back up.

Jake had seen everything collapse around him too.

He stared at Gus's door, noticing each crack, scuff mark, and chip. The Regency was a dump. If he ever wanted to leave this creepy crumbling place, he had to do something.

Jake walked over to the elevator and lifted his eyes from the faded carpet to the kind face of the superintendent. "Danny?"

"Yes, Jake?"

"Were you serious about needing an assistant?"

CHAPTER FIVE

Jake's first few daily rounds had not drastically altered his opinion of the building or its few tenants. But he'd arrived at more of a grudging tolerance. He'd even come up with nicknames for each of his "clients."

"Professor Friendly" didn't even grunt a hello when Jake took away the rotting remains of several noodle-and-chicken dishes.

He jacked the volume on his own headphones every time he delivered mail to Theo "the Racket."

"Sketchball" Delaney kept getting weird fat envelopes dropped off in the mail slot in the front foyer. Jake had delivered a few, and each time, Delaney snapped his fingers and said, "Yo, thanks, dude," before quickly slipping into his apartment with no explanation.

That the name "Delaney" was written on the envelopes in an erratic hand—sometimes with what looked like a crayon—did nothing to calm Jake's suspicions that Sketchball was up to no good.

Gus "the Ghost" still opened the door, but only to reach out his cane to fetch whatever package had arrived for him. He still didn't speak or even grunt thanks.

Lily's cats didn't trust the food Jake put down. They stared at him as if accusing him of being less generous than Danny. He stared back, but when it comes to staring contests, cats are pros. So he ended each visit by sticking out his tongue at her "Finicky Felines."

He didn't have a nickname for Lily herself. Didn't feel right.

But at least the errands kept him out of his apartment and out of his mom's hair.

She still hadn't found a job, or even gotten a nibble.

His mom had cried when Jake told her about his gig, but they were good tears. "Every little bit helps. And to see you growing up?" She'd cried some more and hugged him. He even hugged her back.

He'd also put away his stuff, finally, and done his best to tape the ripped wallpaper back into place. But the apartment still felt small, old, oppressive.

So every morning, Jake woke up, made breakfast while his mom prepped for her day of phone calls, and then left to wait for the mail.

And each day, he would have lunch with Danny, who always seemed happy to talk.

"The Regency was one of a kind when it was built."

"Was that before or after the dinosaurs?" Jake joked.

"Ha-ha. It was the only skyscraper here for a while. Others grew next to it. But a lot of them are crumbling. Not a great part of town."

"Still isn't."

Danny nodded. He began cutting into a cake Delaney had dropped off. "So you still miss the old neighbourhood?" he asked, passing Jake a slice.

Jake looked at the cake, weighing the risk of whatever secret ingredients Sketchball Delaney might have used against his own pangs of hunger. He decided to chance it.

"More each day," he said between bites. The cake was pretty amazing actually.

"Hmm. You must have loved it there. Nice house. Two and a half cars. Big screen TV. Or maybe you spent your time outside? Skateboarding? Baseball?"

Jake didn't answer. Truth was, he didn't spend much time outside if he could help it. Video games, TV shows, watching sports—those were always way more fun, and those happened inside.

Danny moved on. "And I bet you had lots of friends."

Jake stopped chewing. Danny had hit on a sore spot. His "friends." He'd had a bunch—at school and online—but not a single one had called or messaged him since they'd moved. Of course, if he had his computer (or if his old phone did more than play music), he'd probably be able to chat during video games, like normal.

Maybe.

It's not like he expected his friends to visit him—at least not at the Regency. They wouldn't even come to this part of town, he figured, unless it was on a dare. But still, why hadn't they tried to find out how he was doing?

"Yeah. Good crew," Jake said, looking down.

"The people in this place"—Danny pointed to the floors above them—"they can be different. But they have their own kind of charm. They grow on you."

"So does a virus."

Danny chuckled. "I'm starting to like your jokes, Jake."

Jake took another bite of cake. "Why is everybody here a little . . . I dunno, weird?"

"Well, I guess you'd say this isn't a standard apartment building. You don't rent a place here—you sign a special agreement for it."

"Special agreement?"

Danny nodded. "Back when the Regency was built, a lot of people, especially in this part of town, had a hard time finding places to live, places they could afford. There were lots of reasons. Some had simply hit rock bottom. Some had got lost trying to chase a dream. But they all needed help climbing out of a hole."

Jake thought of himself and his mom. "Still people like that."

"True enough. So the deal was—and is—come stay here, contribute what you can as rent, and if you ever hit some kind of success, you give back. But remember that inscription I told you about? Once you're here, you've always got a place to come back to. As long as there's space. That has not been a problem lately."

"What, the economy is too hot?" Jake snorted.

"Ha. No. Too many of the rooms need too much work, so they stay empty. Walls and rugs and floorboards take a lot of abuse over the years."

"I guess that explains why it's so dumpy. Nobody who actually lives here has the cash to help fix things up."

"Ouch!" Danny acted as if Jake had punched him on the arm. "We do our best."

"Sorry. I didn't mean—"

Danny held up his hand. "It's cool, Jake. And it's true. This place has seen better days. But it just needs a chance to . . . well, find its feet again." He looked right at Jake and winked.

Jake started. He had heard his mom use those exact words. "Um . . . feet. Yeah."

The light for 804 lit up.

Danny began wiping his mouth with a napkin, but Jake was already up. He grabbed Gus's package from the table and headed for the door. "Gotta run!"

He also grabbed the last slice of cake.

"Hey!" Danny yelled.

"For the road!"

Jake rode the elevator with a nervous smile. The cake wasn't actually for the road. He'd had an idea.

The elevator dinged for the eighth floor. Jake took a deep breath and marched over to Gus's door. He knocked.

"Gus, I know you're in there." He put his ear against the wood. The muffled sound of a baseball game on the radio. "Is that the Athletics? Their bullpen has been really good this year."

Jake kept his ear to the door for what seemed like an hour. Finally, he heard shuffling noises and the click of the lock.

The door opened a crack. Instead of an arm, a voice. Raspy, as if it hadn't been used in a while. "You like the game?"

"Yeah. I'm not, like, a superfan. But I like it. I watch a lot on TV, or used to."

"Ever play?"

"I played a lot of baseball video games, if that counts."

Gus grunted but didn't say anything.

"Anyway, I have your package and a really amazing slice of cake." Jake put the package and a napkin with the cake on it by the door and stepped away.

The door stayed open. There was a crack from the radio. The announcer's voice rose as the ball flew over the centre field wall for a home run.

"Davis. That guy is amazing," Jake said.

Gus stayed silent.

"Okay. Talk later," Jake said. "Enjoy the game." He waved at the door and walked back to the elevator. "And the cake."

Just before the elevator doors closed, Jake heard a faint voice say, "Thanks."

He felt so good that the rest of his chores passed quickly. He even gave Lily's cats extra snacks.

CHAPTER SIX

A few days later, Jake stepped into the elevator carrying a load of mail, another package for Delaney, and a slice of cake.

"First stop—Gus," Jake said. He reached out to push the button for the eighth floor, then paused. His finger hovered over the buttons for the second and third floors.

Buttons that clearly had never worked, or no longer worked.

He'd pushed them a hundred times. The button for the second floor lit up, but the elevator never stopped there. "You're just mocking me," Jake said after every failed attempt.

The button for the third floor wasn't even real. No matter how hard Jake pushed, it refused to budge. He assumed the crack that ran down the middle had been caused by someone stronger than him, probably Danny, pushing it so hard it broke.

Another mystery, Jake thought. He pushed them anyway, but as the elevator rose, it refused to stop at either floor, and he sighed as he continued from the basement all the way to the eighth.

The elevator opened and Jake got out. He took a deep breath

and carried Gus's package and the piece of cake to apartment 804. He knocked, then sat down on the floor, his back to the wall next to Gus's door.

As he waited for Gus, he smiled. His daily rounds had become something he actually looked forward to. Not just because it got him out of the apartment—and away from his mom, who still hadn't found a job—but because Danny was right. The "clients" grew on you.

The door opened a crack, and Jake slid the package and cake through the gap. The door stayed open, and Jake picked up from where their last conversation had left off.

"Told you the Yankees would come back in that game yesterday."

"The Jays should have taken Smith out before he faced Rodriguez," Gus replied.

Jake laughed. "A hard-throwing lefty pitching to a lefty hitter is usually a good plan."

"The numbers said otherwise. And hard-throwing? Smith's fastball is slower than you delivering my mail." Gus's voice had grown stronger over the last few days.

"Ouch!" Jake said. He had avoided talking anything but baseball to Gus, but for some reason, today felt a little different. "Gus, do you ever think someday we should meet face to face? Maybe actually watch a game?"

Gus took a second to answer. "Don't own a TV. Baseball on the radio is better. And . . . face to face?" He gave a dark chuckle. "I'm fine with this arrangement, kid."

They listened to a few more innings, chatting about stats and strategy, then Jake stood up. "Well, same time tomorrow?"

"Isn't it Sunday? No mail."

"That's true," said Jake. "But there's a doubleheader. I like baseball on the radio too."

"Okay, kid. Okay." Gus slowly slid his door closed as Jake made his way to the elevator and pressed the down button.

He stood in the hallway a second too long, thinking about Gus, and had to jump inside before the doors closed. The sliding iron bar caught one side of his headphones. Jake pulled, and the earbud ripped off completely.

Jake swore. His next stop was Theo, and he used the pounding music in his ears to drown out whatever Theo was pounding out on his piano.

The elevator door slid open on the fifth floor, and Jake jammed the remaining earbud into his right ear and hoped it would be enough.

He walked inside 501, cranking the volume as loud as he could. Rap. Strong beats and loud singing.

"HEY!" Jake yelled.

Theo waved over his shoulder with his right hand but didn't stop noodling around his keyboard with his left.

Jake waved back, even though he knew Theo was lost in his art again. He began organizing the incoming and outgoing mail.

As he stacked up a small pile of envelopes, Jake caught himself moving to the music. Not the rap song. Not Theo's piano music. But the two mixed together. The beat of the song in his ear had somehow made *sense* of the music Theo was playing. The melody, which Jake hadn't picked up in repeated visits to the apartment, joined with the digital loops and made something new. Something Jake could actually follow.

He took the earbud out of his ear, and even without the beat, he could now pick up what Theo was doing.

Theo finished playing with a quick, hard, high *plink*.

Jake gave a loud whoop and applauded.

"Really?" Theo asked, turning around on the piano stool.

"That slapped!"

Theo looked confused. "And that's a good thing?"

"Darn right! But . . . maybe think about adding a beat underneath."

"A beat?"

"I had a song playing in my other ear. Hold on." Jake did his best to tap out the rhythm from his song on the tabletop.

Theo tapped a finger in the air to follow along. "That could definitely work."

Jake gathered up the mail. "Keep at it!"

But Theo had already spun back around and was scribbling some notes on his score sheet. Then he started the song again, this time with a beat softly added in from his right hand. Jake whistled along as he closed the door.

The rest of the day was filled with more surprises. Jake started talking to the other people in the building, and they all started talking back.

The packages for Delaney? Not something sketchy. They were spices and specialized yeasts that he was using in his kitchen.

"Someday I'm going to open my own bakery," he told Jake. "I'm going to call it Carpe Danish."

"Carp what?"

"It means 'seize the danish.' Like the pastry."

"Oh. And you're going to only serve danishes?"

"Nah. It's just a pun. I'll serve lots of stuff. Try these—I made them this morning."

He passed Jake a box filled with mini pies. They smelled amazing.

"Danny is going to love these," Jake said.

Delaney gave him a high five and tied up his apron. It was jet black with a painted silver dragon head covering the front.

"That is cool," Jake said.

Delaney gave a low bow.

The Professor was the next stop. She didn't talk to Jake at first, but when he asked what she was working on, she pointed to an image she'd drawn in chalk of a planet orbiting a large red sun.

"Looks a lot like Earth," Jake said. "Is it the Earth?"

She turned and actually smiled. "Earth-*like*. Orbiting a distant star. My thesis director thinks it's impossible to establish that it's really there. But if I can just figure out the exact—"

She stopped talking and turned away, furiously working on her calculations. Jake scooped up the remains of a couple of boxes of fried chicken and fries, and tossed them in the garbage chute on his way out. They hardly smelled rotten at all, but maybe that was because Jake had started making daily visits.

Irene? The lady who kept forgetting her keys? She turned out to be a writer.

"An idea for a story will just jump into my brain when I least expect it. I have to follow it, so . . ."

"So you sometimes leave your keys in the mailbox or your umbrella by the front door."

Irene nodded. "I have this novel that keeps pushing its way inside my head right now."

"I'd love to read it someday," Jake said, passing her the bag of groceries she'd left in the elevator.

Javier? A cabaret performer. He let Jake try on his latest wig, a mix of sparkles and electric purple streaks.

"You look amazing!" Javier gushed.

Jake's final stop each day was Lily. She'd become, maybe tied with Gus, his favourite person to visit. Not for any reason he could put a finger on. She didn't chat—at all. When Jake arrived, she'd call him Steve and start singing, then he'd shoo the cats into some kind of order and feed them.

Jake had tried to find other ways to help her out. He'd dusted and rearranged photos on the mantelpiece. They were mostly of family, mostly in black and white. One showed a slightly younger Lily surrounded by what Jake assumed were her kids and their families. They were all sitting on the same couch Jake could see in the living room. They were almost all smiling. But not smiling that much. Some of the younger kids seemed bored. Danny had said that Lily had kids and grandkids. But Jake had never seen anyone visit.

One day, when he was dusting, he bumped that picture, revealing a smaller frame behind it. The photo inside the smaller frame was torn and almost completely burned, the edges crinkled and browned. Someone had tried to piece the scraps back together, and Jake thought he could make out the blurry image of a man's face. But he wasn't sure.

Why would anyone keep this? he wondered. But he carefully replaced the frame.

On the walls were hung about four or five framed drawings. They were faded and also slightly scorched. He could just make out the faint pencil lines of some faces, buildings, maybe flowers. He once asked Lily who had made them, but she'd just smiled and laughed and gone back to her song.

Jake ended each visit by making Lily a (not too hot) pot of tea and sitting with her, sipping his own mug.

Lily would always say, "Oh, you are too kind." Or, "What a nice young man. I always knew you'd grow up to be special."

Even if she thought she was saying this to someone named Steve, Jake still felt a swell of pride.

And every once in a while, she'd seem to change slightly, as if she recognized him. This time, after feeding the cats, he smiled at her and she looked straight into his eyes and said, "Did any of it help?"

Jake cocked his head slightly. "Did what?"

But just then, Anastasia leapt onto the table and rubbed against Lily's hand. Lily gave a small smile, petted the cat, and went back to staring into space, singing a song only she knew the words to.

When Jake had finally finished his rounds—and delivered (most of) Delaney's pies to Danny—he found his mom sitting on the sofa doing her nails.

"Guess who's got an in-person interview first thing tomorrow!" she said with a huge smile. She stood up and did a little dance.

Jake ran over and gave her a giant hug.

She looked down at him, running a hand over his head.

"Things are finally looking up."

CHAPTER SEVEN

The sunlight was bright and crisp. The sky a brilliant crystal blue. And Jake could smell his fave breakfast— bacon and eggs with lots of toast and brown butter— wafting from the kitchen.

"Luxury!" he said, taking his seat and immediately stuffing a strip of bacon into his mouth, then another and another.

"Just seemed like maybe it was time to celebrate a little." His mom kissed him on the head, then hurried off to get dressed for her interview. "I've got a good feeling about this one, Jake."

"You'll kill it," Jake said, stuffing his mouth with toast.

His mom closed her bedroom door. Jake looked around his apartment. It seemed brighter. The windows seemed cleaner. The wallpaper more colourful. Less dingy. If his mom got a good job again, they could leave this place. So why didn't he feel happier?

He gulped the last of his OJ and washed the dishes quickly.

"Mom," he called, "I'm gonna get going."

"Okay, Jake. Wish me luck."

"Luck!" He slung his backpack over his shoulder, then

remembered that he'd promised Danny he'd shop for cat food and other supplies after he was done his regular workday.

"I'll be home later than usual," he called.

"Home?"

Jake paused with his hand on the doorknob. "Yeah. Home. For now."

"Love ya."

"Love ya too!"

A few minutes later, Jake almost skipped out of the elevator into the much tidier basement. Danny had used his extra time to clean things up. You could see the floor. Even the narrow bands of light from the windows seemed more brilliant and less grey.

Jake no longer felt he had to be careful where he stepped, and he hurried to tell Danny the good news.

"Mom's got an interview!" he said, beaming as he entered the office.

But Jake's mood changed the second he saw Danny's face. Danny was always smiling, laughing, telling stories. But this morning, he was sitting at the desk, slumped slightly, his head resting in one hand. He barely moved when Jake walked into the office.

"Hey, Supe. What's wrong?"

Danny continued staring straight ahead. Jake thought he heard him moan.

"You sick?" Jake walked over and waved a hand in front of his face. Danny blinked and shook his head like he was waking from a trance.

"Hey, Jake. No, not sick. Just . . . well, look at this." He tapped his finger on a sheet of paper on the desk.

Jake took a seat and turned the paper around to read it. The top had the logo of some lawyer's office in fancy script.

The long-term lease agreement between the Regency and the city expires on the fifteenth of next month.

Attempts to find a new buyer have been unsuccessful. As legal representatives of the Williams estate—Mr. Williams having no immediate family at the time of his death—we have determined with the city that a sale of the land is the best method to retire the debts incurred since Mr. Williams's death.

Jake looked up from the paper. "Mr. Williams?"

"The architect who built and designed this building. A genius. He died a long time ago, and the money he left to keep this place going has run out. Too much going out to pay for upkeep and not enough coming back in. Math."

"Debts? Sale?" Jake wasn't sure he'd read that right, but Danny nodded.

"Keep reading."

Each current resident will receive a lump payment in accordance with the original wording of their individual lease agreement. Demolition is scheduled to commence six months after the posting of this notice, pending review by the city planning department.

That was it. Jake was no lawyer, but he got the gist. The letter was a death sentence for the Regency.

"Can they do this?" he asked.

"It's a building. An old, forgotten, crumbling building, in a city that wants to move on. Maybe they want to build some new glass condo? Or replace it with a parking lot? Not sure."

Danny sighed a deep sigh. "There's a saying my father used to tell me: 'You can't fight city hall.' I'm too old to disagree. Or fight."

"But you keep telling me how special this place is!"

Danny leaned back in his chair and ran his hands over his chin a few times before he spoke. "Jake, you know I love this place. But things change. Even something as solid and beautiful as the Regency. We tried, like a bunch of sailors trying to keep a ship afloat in a storm. But the storm is too strong. The waves too big. The ship is sinking."

Jake fought a rising sense of panic. "Can't we do *something*?"

"Rusting pipes, old mortar, crumbling brick, cracked plaster—those aren't cheap to fix. I'm no millionaire, and no one else here is either. You told me yourself what a dump this place is. The city clearly agrees."

Jake let the paper fall to the desk and stared at it, thinking. "But . . . wait. Where the heck is everyone going to live?"

"Well, the money will help . . . a little. And we'll all just have to find someplace else."

Jake thought of Gus. He never left his apartment. How was he going to find a new place? Delaney might be able to use the money to start his bakery, but Jake suspected not every landlord would see the pastry chef hidden beneath the bike-courier-drug-dealer-dude exterior.

Theo, the Professor, Javier? They relied on him, a kid, to deliver their mail and stop them from getting food poisoning.

Lily?

Jake felt his whole body deflate. Who would take care of her? The cats?

"No. This isn't right."

41

"You and your mom will land on your feet, Jake," Danny said.

Jake closed his eyes and gave his head a shake. He hadn't even thought of himself and his mom. Would they be okay? Probably . . . maybe. But the rest of them?

"Isn't there *anything* we can do?"

"It would take a miracle."

Jake didn't believe in miracles, and he could see by the frown on Danny's face that he didn't either.

Just then, a red light flashed over Danny's head. The bulb for 702.

"Delaney's home?" Jake stood to go see what he needed, but Danny put up a hand to stop him.

"I'll go. I need to feel useful." He patted Jake's shoulder before shuffling slowly out the door.

Jake sat back down and tried to figure out what he was actually feeling. Confused? Certainly. His mom had said they could make a home here. It had just started feeling like a home, of sorts. Now, like his old home, it was about to be taken away. Hope had flickered like a flash of lightning . . . and was vanishing just as quickly.

Jake leaned on his elbows. Then he punched his hands down on the table, hard.

Something metal clanked. He stood up and looked behind the phone. Danny had left his keys. Jake leaned over and scooped them up.

"Danny!" he called. There was no answer. Danny must have already left in the elevator for the seventh floor.

If Delaney's home, he won't need them anyway, Jake thought. He sat back down and looked around at the oak panels lining the

walls of the office. It was a beautiful, strange place. Did demolition crews save stuff like these panels? Or just crush it to dust
with bulldozers before dumping it?

He got up and ran his hands along the smooth wood. "Sorry,
pal," he said to the building.

A red light flashed across his fingers.

He looked up.

The red light on the wall flashed again.

"What the . . . ?"

It wasn't Delaney or Gus or Lily.

It was apartment 713.

Jake got on his tiptoes, peering at the board to make sure.

The light blinked on and off, growing brighter each time.
The layers of ancient tape came loose and floated to the ground
one by one.

"Danny?" Jake called, not sure what to do. "DANNY?"

No answer.

This made no* sense. Apartment 713 was empty. It was
off-limits. Danny had said so. Jake closed his eyes and opened
them, but the red light flashed even brighter.

"Okay. Think, Jake, think. Danny is on the seventh floor
already. He's helping Delaney with something. Maybe he went
into 713 to test the button and got locked in? And he needs me to
come open the door. That must be it."

Jake clutched the keys and sped to the elevator. It was already
waiting for him, doors open.

He jumped in and pressed the number 7. He caught his
reflection in the mirrors. He was shaking. All the Jakes were
shaking. Why was he shaking?

The doors opened into an empty hallway. Jake crept out.

"Danny? Delaney?" His voice echoed off the walls. No one answered.

He knocked on Delaney's door. No answer. He heard a faint hum and leaned his ear to the door. But the hum wasn't from Delaney's apartment. It was coming from across the hall.

Apartment 713.

Jake turned and walked up to the door. The hum was very low, from deep inside. He leaned an ear against the wood. It felt warm. His toes felt warm too. Jake looked down. A weak strip of yellowish light now snuck out from underneath. It spread bit by bit across the floor and up the door.

The places where the light hit seemed less worn, less marked up. The brass doorknob was suddenly shinier. The tattered wallpaper around the doorframe seemed to have been repaired and cleaned.

"This is weird," Jake whispered. He raised his hand to knock, keys clutched between his trembling fingers. Then he heard voices from inside. Talking excitedly. Arguing. Then scuffling feet followed by glass crashing to the ground.

Jake called for Danny again, but there was no answer. Should he go look for him? Was Danny inside? Was he in trouble?

Suddenly, there was a loud crash and a cry of "HELP! OH, HELP ME!" from inside. "HELLLLLPPPP!"

Someone needed something, and it was up to Jake to see who and what that was.

He jammed the key in the lock and turned it.

The door swung open, pulling Jake along with it. He stumbled onto a carpeted floor as the door slammed shut behind him.

Oh no! He'd left the keys in the lock. He reached back and grabbed the doorknob. He pulled and pulled, but it refused to open!

An even louder scream from deep inside the apartment made the hairs on his neck stand up. He'd made a terrible mistake. He'd thought he could help, but now *he* was trapped. "Jake, you doofus," he said.

Footsteps.

He didn't dare turn around. The door refused to open. Danny had told him not to go into apartment 713, and he was about to find out the horrible reason why.

The footsteps stopped right behind him. A hand touched his shoulder.

Jake jumped so high he almost knocked his head on the ceiling. He spun around, eyes closed, pushing his back against the door, expecting the end.

"Please don't kill me!"

There was a tapping noise and then a girl's voice.

"Kill you? Who in the Sam Hill *are* you?"

CHAPTER EIGHT

Jake opened his eyes. Instead of an axe-wielding murderer, he was face to face with a girl his own age. She was wearing an emerald-green dress and tapping shiny black shoes on the floor, arms crossed and head cocked to one side.

"I asked you a question," said the girl, now poking at his chest with her finger. "Spill."

"Spill?"

"Yeah, spill. Start with answering this: Who are you?"

Jake relaxed a little. "Sorry. I'm Jake. I just moved in upstairs. I help out with the superintendent. I heard a scream—"

"Superintendent?" She raised an eyebrow.

"Yeah. Danny? Don't you know him?"

"Danny," the girl repeated slowly, tilting her head even more. "And what apartment did you say you moved into?"

"Um, 901. Me and my mom."

The girl pursed her lips and nodded but kept her eyes locked on Jake.

"Sorry," Jake said, "I didn't ask your name."

She looked Jake up and down before answering. "Beth. This is my home, and I'm not very impressed with some hinky young man barging in unannounced."

"Hinky?"

"Definitely hinky."

Jake had no idea what the word meant, but it was clearly not a good thing.

"Look, Beth, I apologize for barging in. But I heard a scream, and I was just coming to help."

"Help?" She glared at Jake. "Applesauce."

"Applesauce? What does that even mean?"

"It means I don't believe you. No one here asked for help."

Jake felt a rising annoyance fighting with his fear. "Listen, Beth. The light in the basement came on. I had the keys. Danny wasn't around and . . . and . . . I HEARD A SCREAM!"

Beth gave a quick snort. "Ha! That was some dame named Petunia, on the *radio*. She'd just been kidnapped by pirates. I happen to *love* pirates. But she didn't, so she screamed. I turned it off when I heard a young ruffian breaking into my apartment."

"I didn't break—"

"AND SO, thanks to you, I'll never find out what happened to her!" Beth glared at Jake.

"Why don't you just download it and listen to it later?" Jake asked.

Beth looked at him like he'd just sprung antlers. "Load down . . . what?"

"Download. Sounds like you were listening to a podcast or something."

"Podcast?" Beth leaned close to Jake's face and peered into his eyes. "Who. Are. You. Really?"

"I'm Jake. Jake Simmons. Just like I said."

"Apartment 901." Beth nodded, then she took a step back and pointed at his clothes. "What is that getup?"

Jake looked down at his blue jeans and grey sweatshirt. "Um. Clothes."

"Do you work in a factory or on a farm or something?"

"Work? No. It's a hoodie."

"You're a hood! So you robbed a bank? On the lam?"

"Lamb?" Jake gave his head a shake. No wonder Danny had told him to stay away from this apartment. Beth was clearly a little funny in the head. Whatever "help" they needed here in apartment 713, he was not equipped to provide it.

"Maybe I should leave," Jake said. "I'll go get Danny and he can give you whatever help you and your friend Petunia need."

Beth crossed her arms and smiled. "Okay, go ahead and leave." She waved her hand toward the door, smirking.

Jake frowned at the door—the door he'd already been unable to open. "Um, yeah. The keys must have got stuck in the other side and jammed the lock."

"The keys you got from Danny. Danny the superintendent." Beth nodded, a smile dancing on her lips. "You know what's funny, Jake from apartment 901? There is no superintendent, and the only Danny I know is the soda jerk down the street."

"Danny's not a jerk."

"Your imaginary friend isn't a jerk. Fine. Good. Now it's really time to go."

Beth took a step toward Jake, and he braced for some kind of attack. But instead of stabbing him or punching him, she reached for a small knot in the wooden doorframe just above his left ear. She pushed.

There was a click and the door opened.

"Nice little security measure from Mr. Williams. Hard to spot unless you know it's there. A robber comes in when the apartment is empty, but then he can't get out." She pulled Jake a step toward her, then reached over and opened the door.

"Mr. Williams?" The name rang a bell.

"Yes. Mr. Williams. This is his building, and he takes care of everything. Including the ninth floor, which I didn't know he'd even opened. And because he takes care of everything, there's no need for a superintendent. Now, on your way." Beth gave Jake a gentle shove and he staggered backward into the hallway.

"Wait, you're talking about the guy who built this place? What is he—a ghost?"

"Goodbye, Jake from apartment 901." Beth closed the door.

Jake snorted. "Yeah, goodbye and good riddance."

He reached for the keys, but they weren't in the lock. The polished brass lock under the shiny doorknob on the unscuffed wooden door. Which was surrounded by brightly coloured wallpaper.

"What the heck?" It was like someone had snuck in and replaced all the old stuff with newer and better versions. Jake touched the door, half expecting it to disappear. But it was solid and smooth.

A laugh from his left broke his concentration. The laugh was followed by voices. Lots of voices. Jake turned and watched in confusion as at least six people stood waiting for the elevator. A woman in a long dress closed the door to apartment 711 and joined them.

But 711 was empty, wasn't it?

49

As far as he knew, Delaney was the only one who lived on this floor. Well, now he knew Beth did too.

What was going on? Were these the developers from the city? Demolition experts, maybe? Already? Why were they dressed in such weird clothes? Halloween was months away.

One of the men saw Jake watching them. "It's not polite to stare, scout."

Scout? Jake shook his head. "Um. Sorry, sir."

But he continued to stare despite himself. The suits and dresses weren't like other suits and dresses he'd seen. These were big, baggy, sparkly. One of the women coughed, and Jake forced himself to look at the carpet.

Which seemed brand new. Not a single rip or worn patch.

He caught snippets of their strange conversation.

"Some low-down egg dinged my roadster."

"That guy is bad medicine."

"He's my best chum!"

What the heck were they talking about?

The elevator arrived, and the doors slid noiselessly apart.

Noiselessly? No grind of metal? No creak of old gears? When did Danny have time to oil it?

Jake looked back up.

"Have a good day, son." The man tipped his large-brimmed brown hat and stepped through the doors.

Tipped his hat? And who wore hats like *that*?

"How the h—" Jake began, but he didn't know what he wanted to say next. He shook his head. Something was wrong. Something was messed up. This wasn't the Regency. At least not the Regency he lived in. The one he'd come to know. The one with Danny, Lily, Gus, Theo, and—

"Mom!" Jake ran to the stairway. The carpet beneath his sneakers was so plush, it swallowed the sound of his footsteps. The floorboards didn't creak or groan. No puffs of decades-old dust followed his every step.

He took the stairs three at a time, slammed opened the door to the ninth floor, and stopped cold.

The hallway floor was bare wood.

The walls were white plaster.

The doors to apartment 901 and all the other apartments on his floor . . . were gone.

CHAPTER NINE

Jake walked quietly into what was supposed to be his kitchen. The walls were bare. There was a sink but no stove. No fridge. No cupboards. No chipped and worn tiles. No Mom. "Mom?" he called out. His voice echoed around the walls of the empty space.

Jake's footsteps sounded impossibly loud as he walked from room to empty room. There was no wallpaper in his bedroom, faded or new. His head spun, filled with questions he could barely articulate, let alone try to answer.

How long had he been gone? Had he been drugged and kept hostage? Had his mom abandoned him? Renovated their apartment and moved?

He heard strange noises coming from outside. The neighbourhood was usually so quiet. He walked over to the window. The glass was covered in stiff brown paper tacked to the corners of the unpainted wooden frame. Jake peeled a corner and peeked out. He hoped he'd see his mom—or Danny, or a moving van—pulled up on the cracked concrete of the sidewalk.

But the sidewalks far below weren't cracked. They were smooth. No shoots of weeds rose up between the concrete squares.

And there were so many people walking around! The men all seemed to be wearing the same dark suits and wide-brimmed hats as the men he'd seen in the hallway. The women were in long dresses. Some wore feathers in their bowl-shaped caps.

There was a loud honk and Jake saw the cars. Not the rusty old cars that he sometimes saw outside the Regency when he collected the mail, but shiny black ones with large thin tires and dark cloth tops. He'd once taken a ride in something similar at a carnival, on metal tracks. Was there a fair in town?

The honks were joined by neighs, and Jake watched as a line of horse-drawn carriages turned the corner below. People on bikes wove in and out around them. No one wore a helmet or funny-looking bike shorts like the ones his mom and Janice used to wear.

There was a low rumble, and a trolley car moved slowly down the middle of the road. People jumped on and off as the car slowed to a crawl at the street corner.

He gave his head a shake. Maybe someone was filming a movie on their block? But how did they set it up so fast? He hadn't heard any workers outside this morning.

A pigeon flashed across the window, and Jake followed its flight. His jaw fell. The buildings that had flanked the Regency were gone, replaced by a horizon filled with church steeples, tall trees, flocks of birds—and in the distance, smokestacks releasing thick grey clouds into the air.

Was he dreaming?

Was he hallucinating?

He turned and leaned his back against the wall, then slid down until he was on the floor, cradling his legs tightly against his body. His brain raced to make sense of what he was seeing, hearing, feeling.

He'd eaten some of Delaney's latest pies a couple of days before. Maybe they had some funny secret ingredients in them? But this all felt, sounded, and seemed so real.

It *couldn't* be real, though. It was too weird, too strange. If he just closed his eyes, he would be back in his room. In his own room. His room at the Regency. He'd never wanted that so much. He closed his eyes so tightly he could feel his eyeballs squeeze against the lids. He curled into a ball on the floor and fell into a deep sleep.

Click.

Click.

Click.

Jake woke to the sound of steps on the wooden floor. He raised his head slowly and wiped a streak of spittle from his lips and cheek. How long had he been out?

The steps drew closer.

"Mom?" Jake opened his eyes.

It was Beth who leaned over him.

"Hmm," she said, tapping her feet. "So this is your apartment? Nice place. Where's your family? Your stuff?"

Jake forced himself into a sitting position. His mouth felt dry and his head was still foggy. "I'm telling you this is where I live. They must be renovating the apartment, and my mom moved out while they do the work." *Or she had to go so they could rip it down piece by piece*, he thought.

"Uh-huh." Beth stood up and crossed her arms. "See, here's the problem—this floor isn't finished because it's not going to be finished. Mr. Williams has stopped work on the building ever since . . ."

"Since what?"

Beth pursed her lips and shook her head. "Doesn't matter. I'm just telling you that no one has ever lived on this floor, and until things change, no one ever will."

"But I DO."

Beth frowned. "Look, Jake. I know what kind of people show up in this building. People who don't always have another place to go. You don't need to lie to me."

"I'm not lying! And I know that's why people live here. I told you, I help Danny keep this dump from falling down."

"Dump?" She frowned.

"Sorry," he said. "I know. It's a 'hidden gem.' Or it used to be."

"Used to be?"

"I'm sure it was lovely once. Danny keeps telling me that. Mom too, sort of."

"That's not what I meant—"

Jake kept talking. "And I assume if you're here, you also don't have any other options, right?"

Beth winced. "Not exactly." She took a long, deep breath and spoke so quietly Jake had to strain to hear her. "My father was one of the workers on the building when it was first going up."

"Was?"

Beth looked away out the window. "Never mind. Mr. Williams let us stay, and that's all that matters."

Jake could tell there was more to this story and was about to ask what it was when Beth turned back to face him. Her lips were thin and tight, but even still, they trembled slightly. Something in her eyes told Jake to let it drop.

"Here." She held out a square covered in waxed paper. "I figured you might need this."

Jake hesitated.

Beth unfolded a corner of the paper, revealing a slice of deep brown bread. "There's only a little poison. It's mostly peanut butter and jelly."

Jake still hesitated.

"That was a joke, Jake." She folded the paper back and held out the sandwich again. "My mom made the bread and the jelly, so one wrong word and I'll pop you."

"Okay! Okay!" Jake held up his hands in surrender. His stomach grumbled. How could he be so hungry? Maybe that was the answer! He'd banged his head and had been unconscious for hours, or maybe days. He hadn't eaten because he'd been out cold. He grabbed the sandwich and began wolfing it down.

"Slow down!" Beth said. "If you swallow the paper, it'll block you like a sewer."

Jake didn't want to know how Beth knew that. He was able to push out a "Thanks, this is really good" between bites. He licked his fingers and smiled. "The poison adds a certain *je ne sais quoi*." He blew a chef's kiss.

"Ha-ha. You're a real riot, Jake. Now we should try to get you some real clothes too."

"What's wrong with my clothes?"

Beth snorted. "What's right with them? Dirty dungarees? No hat? Those weird shoes? You look like you escaped from some

56

factory or something. Maybe you did. One look at that getup and the coppers'll send you back—or throw you in the clink."

"The what? Factory?"

Beth tapped a finger on her lips. "Or maybe you're from some other country? Might explain all the weird words you use."

"*I* use weird words? I was born, like, an hour's drive from here. Maypole Woods. Just google it!"

"Yeah, weird words like that. But don't worry! If you need to kip here for a bit"—she took in the apartment with a wave of her hand—"your secret is safe with me."

"I LIVE HERE."

Beth winked. "Sure, kiddo." She turned to leave but called back over her shoulder, "And don't call the Regency a dump again. It's a palace. A shining new wonderful palace."

Jake slumped back against the wall, completely confused. His clothes were wrong? A factory? Weird words?

Then two things Beth had said finally struck him: "my father was one of the workers" and "new." Beth was the same age he was, or pretty darned close. How old was her dad? How old was the Regency?

"No," he whispered to the empty room. "No. No. No."

It wasn't that the idea hadn't occurred to Jake as soon as he'd arrived. It's just that it had seemed absolutely impossible.

He ran to the window. There was no movie being filmed. Those were old cars. No, *new* cars. There were no big buildings because they hadn't been built yet. There was no Mom because she hadn't been born yet. Danny hadn't been born yet. *He* hadn't been born yet. So how was he here?

Jake suddenly felt dizzy. He leaned his hands on the walls and fought the urge to throw up.

He hobbled over to the kitchen sink. Luckily, the pipes in this *new* unfinished apartment had been connected. He splashed cold water on his face. He had no idea how it had happened. How it *could* happen. But the moment he'd entered apartment 713, he'd stepped into . . . *whenever* it was now.

He needed to get back home. But how?

He needed to go back inside apartment 713.

CHAPTER TEN

You're screwy," Beth said, and she started to close the door in his face.

Jake pushed back, speaking quickly through the shrinking crack. "I'm not. I'm telling you, somehow I've been sent back in time, to when the building was almost new."

"Two minutes ago, you were telling me that you and your mom live in 901."

"I know. And we do . . . or did . . . or will. I'm not sure how this is all happening. But the moment I came into this room, everything changed to . . . um, what year is it?"

Beth narrowed her eyes. "Stop joking."

"I'm not. I have no idea what's going on, but I need to get back to my own version of this building, whenever that is."

"That's why you made that weird comment about the radio play?"

"So you can't save it and play it back later?"

"Save? Like, record it on a phonograph?"

Jake had no idea what a phonograph was. He was about to

explain how his own music apps worked, but a nagging voice in the back of his head made him stop. The voice belonged to his mom's girlfriend—or ex-girlfriend, or future girlfriend—Janice. She and his mom had gone to see a movie about time travel. They'd talked about it over dinner. He was in the middle of a video game so had only paid a little attention. But one bit of their conversation now came back to him.

"Changing the past can change the future. For good *and* for bad," Janice said. "It's called the butterfly effect. Even a small change in the past can completely alter the future. And maybe make it worse. You gotta be careful messing with time."

"What could really happen?" his mom joked.

Jake remembered that Janice had leaned close to her and said, in as serious a voice as she could, "Talking dinosaurs in armoured tanks."

His mom had laughed—a sound he missed so much it hurt— and he'd gone back to his video game.

What if telling Beth the truth about technology was the exact wrong thing to do? Janice had been joking about the dinosaurs, but other bad stuff could happen.

Jake still had absolutely zero idea what, if anything, he was supposed to be doing here. But he was pretty sure his mission didn't include telling Beth about digital music files.

Even though he'd already let the cat out of the bag that he was from the future, Beth clearly didn't believe him, so Jake decided to play it safe for a bit. "Yeah. Like a recording. Where I come from, almost anyone can make one. Then you can listen any time."

"Well, Jake, that only shows you have a very active imagination. I'd like some proof."

He searched his pockets for anything that might prove his story. But apart from a few crumbs and the remains of some tissues, he had nothing.

"No foreign coins? Or money from the year 3025?" Beth said.

Jake gave an exasperated grunt. "Look, your apartment is special somehow."

"Of course it is. I live here." She grinned.

"I mean that all this started when I unlocked your door and fell inside. I need to see why I'm here."

"My apartment is the same as all the others. And my mom *isn't* here, so no way." She gave one final push, and the door closed with a click.

Jake leaned his head against the jamb. "Beth, if you don't help me figure this out, you can kiss this wonderful palace of yours goodbye. The Regency is in trouble."

He held his breath and listened. There was a click as Beth reopened the door a crack.

"What do you mean?"

"The Regency. It's about to be torn down."

"It's just been built. That's the craziest thing you've said so far."

Jake hung his head. "In my home time, it's a dump. It's about to be sold. The city is going to tear it down and kick everyone out."

Beth paused, biting her lip, thinking. Then she shook her head. "Mr. Williams would never let that happen."

Before Jake could respond, a deep voice said, "Did I hear someone call my name?"

Jake turned slowly. A tall man packed into a tan suit that

seemed ready to burst at the seams was leaning against the wall, smiling at him.

"I don't think I've seen you before, young man. My name is Jeremiah Williams. And this 'dump,' as you called it, is my life's work."

Jake gulped. Danny had told him that Williams was a genius. What he'd failed to mention was that he was built like a bulked-up superhero. And Jake had just insulted his pride and joy.

"Hi, Jeremiah," Jake said, doing his best to force a smile.

"You can call me Mr. Williams."

"Um, okay, Mr. Williams. My name is Jake Simmons. I didn't mean the Regency is a dump *now*. I meant that it could turn into one if—"

He struggled to say something that wouldn't sound insulting. A quick look at the architect's face showed he was failing. Jake stopped smiling and composed himself. He tried to explain again.

"Mr. Williams, I love this place. I do." He paused for a second. Was that the truth? He continued, "I love the hidden elevator. I love the weird garbage chutes, the secret buttons that get you into the basement office—"

Williams cocked his head. "How do you know about that?"

Jake's mind raced. He needed to say something that wouldn't, as Beth had warned, get him kicked out of the building, or sent to jail or some factory. "I . . . I've been looking around."

"Looking around?"

"My mom and I need a place to stay. She's been having trouble finding work."

Williams bowed his head. "Go on."

"Mom heard about this place and then I decided to scout it out. Beth was helping me."

She snorted from the doorway.

Williams raised an eyebrow. "Beth, do you know this boy? Or was he bothering you?"

"He was definitely bothering me," she said.

Jake shot her a pleading look and mouthed "Please."

She thought for a second, then continued, "But I know him. He's my . . . distant cousin. He's bunking with us while his mom looks for a place to stay. We just had a . . . disagreement. So I locked him out."

Jake gave Beth a beaming smile.

Williams relaxed his muscles and his smile returned. "Well, that is a horse of a completely different colour." With a noticeable limp, he walked over to Jake and held out his hand. "Welcome to my home, Jake Simmons."

Jake's own hand disappeared as Williams shook it vigorously.

"So you've been sneaking—I mean looking—around my building? Anything I should know?"

Jake wondered if there was anything Williams didn't know. "Well," he began, "I can tell you that the door to the fourth floor can swing open too fast if someone opens a door above it. Not sure why. The wind or something."

Williams nodded. "Good to know."

"And there's a leak in the boiler line that runs to the radiators on the west side of the building."

"That just got installed last year!"

"Maybe keep an eye on it. And for some reason, the ninth floor is unfinished."

Williams made a pained expression, but it passed quickly. "What about the Great Hall?"

"Great Hall?" Jake had never heard of it.

Williams winked. "It looks like it's my turn to surprise you, Jake. There's a concert there tonight, and I've sold a lot of tickets for people who want to see Louis."

"Looey?"

"Louis Armstrong," Williams said. "He blows a mean horn."

"And he's playing here? At an apartment building?"

Williams's face broke into a huge smile. "You think the Regency is just an apartment building? You've clearly never snuck onto the second floor."

Jake shook his head. "No, sir."

"Or into the kitchen?"

"There's a kitchen?"

"This sounds like an opportunity to provide you with a little architectural education." Williams walked slowly toward the elevator and motioned for Jake to join him.

"Mr. Williams," Jake said, "can I just grab my hat from the apartment first?"

"Sure, but make it quick. Mr. Armstrong is about to practise." Williams held the door to the elevator. "Beth," he said, "you wanna come too? I know how much the place means to you."

She nodded silently.

"Can I please have a quick look inside before we go?" Jake whispered to Beth.

She rolled her eyes but stepped aside. "You have thirty seconds."

Jake sprinted around the inside of apartment 713. Each time he ran into or out of a room, he hoped something would happen—a zap back to the present or some sign or clue about why he was here in the past—but nothing did.

It was exactly the same layout as his apartment but filled with furniture, a radio, carpets, and beds. Framed drawings of angels and animals hung from nails in the wall.

"They get to use nails?!" he said to himself. "Unfair."

Jake hung his head. If the answer to his mystery was somewhere in this apartment, it was truly hidden.

"I was hoping this would be easier," he said under his breath.

He walked back to the door and opened and closed it repeatedly. Each time, Beth was there in the hallway, looking more and more annoyed.

"Enough," she finally said, sticking her foot in the doorway. "Time to go."

Jake shuffled past her, and they made their way into the elevator.

"Where's your hat?" asked Williams.

"I have absolutely no idea," Jake answered.

Williams chuckled. "I've never seen anyone look so low over a *hat* before. But maybe this trip will cheer you up."

The elevator door closed.

CHAPTER ELEVEN

Williams put an arm around Beth's shoulder and gave a squeeze. Jake wondered why she was being so quiet all of a sudden. He'd only just met her and "quiet" was not an adjective he'd use to describe her.

Instead of pushing the button for the second floor, Williams pulled a long chain out of his vest pocket. At the end was a gold watch and a thin key. He began to put the key against the button for the third floor.

"Oh, that button is cracked. It doesn't work," Jake said.

"I know," Williams said. "Unless you have this." The key slid into the crack in the glass, and the button instantly lit up. "It takes me to my private balcony. Can't get in there without this key. Bet you didn't know about that," he said with a wink.

Jake didn't, but Danny had told him the Regency was filled with secrets, and it felt nice to have one all to himself. Well, all to himself and Beth.

He thought of the basement office and wondered what a private balcony designed by Williams might look like.

The elevator opened onto a darkened room. A light flickered and the floor shone like glass.

"Marble," Williams said. "The pillars too."

"Pillars?" Jake asked.

He stepped into the room. On either side of the elevator door, pillars covered in carved vines (of course) rose up, disappearing into darkness.

"What's up there?" Jake asked.

"This." Williams hit a switch hidden somewhere among the vines.

The room was flooded with light. Jake had to momentarily shield his eyes. When he opened them again, he couldn't help but stare in wonder.

The gold-painted ceiling shimmered like water under a rising sun. Two arches grew from the top of each pillar, rising up and then seeming to fly away through the far wall. They formed a giant *V* right overhead. More twisting, elegant vines scrolled along the length of each arch, branching into golden leaves and bunches of grapes.

"OMG," Jake said.

"Oh *what*?" Beth asked.

"It just means wow."

"Thank you," said Williams. "The one drawback is that the glorious ceiling can prevent visitors from noticing the walls."

Jake now noticed. The walls were oak, like the walls in the basement, but the panels here were even more intricately decorated. Carved animal heads, so lifelike Jake could almost hear them breathe, held watch over an odd array of dollhouse-sized doors.

Each door had a brass keyhole and handle.

"We think it's kind of a filing cabinet," Williams said, gently running his hand over a carved lion.

"Think?"

Williams nodded, then pushed the animal's nose. Its mouth opened wide, revealing a red velvet tongue. He reached a finger inside and pulled out an ornate silver key. The handle was embossed with a picture of an empty flowerpot.

"What's that for?" Jake asked.

"I have no idea." Williams placed the key back into the lion's mouth and gently tapped the lower jaw back in place. "I've tried it on all the keyholes I could find in this room, but so far I have not discovered a match."

"So you don't know what's behind all these doors?"

"Some of them open. I keep blueprints, files, things like that inside. But the rest remain closed to me. To us, actually."

Jake ran his hands over the carved mouldings, pushing more noses, tugging ears, shaking paws, but nothing else popped open. "Did you make these, Mr. Williams?" he asked.

There was an awkward silence, and Jake saw Williams and Beth exchange a look.

"The original designs were mine, but the man who made these far exceeded my humble scribbles."

Beth sniffed and wiped her eyes on her sleeve.

The pieces started to fit together like a puzzle.

"Your dad made all these carvings, didn't he?" Jake asked.

Beth nodded.

69

"Beth's father, Charles, was an amazing artist and a close friend," Williams said. "I only had to describe my vision to him, and he would take it and make . . ." He held his hands up, taking in the whole room. "He would make magic. I admit it has been very difficult to continue the work without him."

Jake stared around in wonder. He'd never been in such a cool place. "This is all so amazing."

Williams bowed his head. "Thank you, Jake Simmons. It is certainly a great seat for all the shows, and a quiet retreat when you need a place to escape."

"And imagine what could be hidden in all these drawers!" Jake said.

Beth smiled. "Father loved games and riddles. He told me you could spend a lifetime trying to find all the secrets hidden in the Regency and never succeed."

"Wow."

Beth sighed. "Before he died, he told me that he'd buried a treasure somewhere in here. He wanted us to look for it."

"We've looked," Williams said with a shrug. "And we've never been able to find anything but the key with no lock." He pulled out his watch and checked the time. "The rehearsal is about to start."

Jake gazed at the four walls. "Can't we stay here a little longer?"

"Oh, there's no need to leave!" Williams smiled. "I said this was a great seat."

"Get ready," Beth said, sidling up to Jake.

"Allow me to show you our true masterpiece," Williams said.

"It's not this?" Jake asked, stunned.

"This room is only the opening act."

"Or the un-opening act," Jake joked, pointing at the keyholes on the wall.

Williams chuckled, but Beth snorted.

"I thought people from the future would have better jokes," she whispered to Jake.

Williams walked over to the far wall, where he shook the paw of an enormous bear. There was the whir of invisible gears as the panels slid sideways and the wall disappeared.

Jake gasped.

It was as if Williams had opened the gates to a majestic dragon's lair filled with piles of stolen coins and gems. The summer sun sent shafts of golden light through giant windows. The gilded ceiling glowed like it had been set on fire.

Williams beamed. "The Great Hall is, in some ways, an enlarged version of the room where we now stand. But it is so much more."

"No kidding," said Jake, walking slowly forward. There was more gold, more carvings, more soaring space. Two larger arches spread across the ceiling like the ribs of a great whale, rising higher and higher, then crossing over each other in the middle before descending to the far walls.

The sun bathed Williams in light, and as he stood against the balcony, he glowed. Jake almost expected him to sprout wings and fly away.

A high clear trumpet blast filled the hall.

Wait, Jake thought. *What if I've died, and this is heaven?* He shuddered. "Beth, can you pinch me to make sure I'm real?"

She chuckled, then pinched him so hard he winced. "You're real. A real goof."

Williams leaned over the balcony and waved. "Ah! Mr. Armstrong! Is all in order?"

"You know it, boss," came a raspy voice. "Getting in some practice to hear the way this beautiful room talks. Just about to try something out with the band. Want to have a listen?"

Williams turned his head. "Children?"

Beth nodded vigorously. "I've heard him on the radio. He's tops. Mom even has a few records."

Jake was too mesmerized by the wonders around him to answer.

"Jake?" Beth's voice broke his trance for a moment. "Come over and listen."

He nodded dumbly and walked to the railing, looking for some kind of slot or opening into which the wall panels had disappeared. But if a slot was there, it was invisible.

Why had Danny never shown him this? He thought of the key Williams had used to get in here. It wasn't like any of the ones on Danny's keychain. Maybe Danny didn't know about this place?

Jake was so lost in thought that he hadn't registered the trills and scales coming from the hall below until he began tapping his toes and humming along. Armstrong and his band were warming into their song. It was similar to the music Theo "the Racket" had been composing on his piano.

At first listen, it had struck Jake as just noise. But like Theo's music, it began to make sense to him the more he listened. He could hear the way Armstrong was taking a series of notes, then turning them upside down, then playing them backward, then forward again. The other members of the band picked up on the pattern on their instruments, making their own changes.

Beth tapped his shoulder. "Your mouth is open."

Jake smiled and continued tapping the railing in time with the rhythm.

Armstrong and his bandmates were wearing suits like the ones he'd seen on the men in the hallway. They moved and swayed slightly as they played drums, bass, piano, and trumpet.

Beth beamed. "Isn't he a humdinger!"

Jake nodded. Armstrong was now walking around the stage, pointing his horn at different parts of the hall. Then he'd stop and listen for the reverberation. He gave a huge smile and waved his hand at Williams. "This place sounds just as wonderful as it looks," he said. "As good a venue as we've ever played."

Williams gave a low bow. "Can't wait to hear the actual concert tonight."

Armstrong blew a loud trill on his horn, then waved to his band. "All right, time to grab some grub. Bye, Jeremiah!"

"I suggest Antoine's for dinner," Williams replied. "Tell him I sent you."

Beth leaned over to Jake. "Antoine got his start here," she whispered, "making dinners for big parties."

"Worth a visit?"

Beth laughed. "Unless you actually *did* rob a bank, there's zero chance we're ever eating at Antoine's."

"Well, children, I've got some work to do," Williams said,

shaking the bear's paw again. The panels slid back into place, and the wall once again enclosed the balcony. The sunlight disappeared, but the balcony still glowed, as if a tiny bit had been trapped behind the walls and was dancing among the animals and leaves.

"Thank you, Mr. Williams," Beth said.

Jake was speechless. He stared again in wonder at the room, the architect, and the girl whose father had helped make all this.

What was he doing here? With them? He had a sudden vision of his mother searching the hallways, frantically calling his name. Danny knocking on doors, looking for him.

He'd been here for only a few hours, but he'd accepted that this was real. That he was, somehow, in the past.

He had no idea why, though, or what he was supposed to do. But it had to have something to do with the Regency and the two people standing in front of him now, staring at him. He hadn't found an answer in Beth's apartment, but he hadn't looked that closely either.

Or maybe the secrets were hidden somewhere, like so many secrets of the Regency. He needed to keep searching. He needed to find a way to stay and search.

His stomach rumbled. He also needed to eat.

"Jake? You okay?" Beth looked genuinely worried.

Jake nodded. He had an idea. He shook Williams's hand. "Thanks for showing me this place. It's amazing. And, Mr. Williams, can I ask you a question?"

"Of course."

"Do you ever need any help around here?"

Williams thought for a moment. "Now that you mention it . . ."

CHAPTER TWELVE

s it turned out, Williams said he could use TWO helpers.
And the next morning, Beth and Jake were together,
sweeping up a concert floor covered with ticket stubs,
confetti, bits of burst balloons, paper scraps, and a tremendous
amount of popcorn and peanut shells.

"Who watched this concert? Elephants?" Jake asked, pushing a pile of shells with his broom.

Beth ignored him. "Wasn't he amazing?" she asked.

"The first part was, until Mr. Williams told us it was time to
head to bed." Jake dumped the garbage into a metal waste bin.
He'd searched every nook and cranny around the stage, finding
nothing to help answer the question "Why am I here?"

Beth had finally told him to cut it out and get to work.

"Don't be a wet noodle. And it was super nice of Mr. Williams
to let us meet Mr. Armstrong during intermission," she said.

"He even got him to sign an album sleeve for me!"

"I thought you didn't know what that was?"

"Well, I do *now*." The sleeve itself was nothing more than the paper covering for one of Armstrong's records. But Armstrong had signed "Best wishes to a real crackerjake" with a flourish.

The hall looked different in the morning light. Still beautiful, but softer somehow. Light crept, more than poured, through the tall windows, bathing the entire ballroom in silver. Dust floated like snow in the sunbeams. The ceiling, which had seemed high from the balcony, appeared from the floor to be as unreachable as the sky.

Beth began dancing with her broom in time to one of the songs from the night before. She hummed the tune and reached her hand out for Jake to join her.

Jake shook her off. "Turns out sleeping on the floor isn't the best thing for a back." He rolled his shoulders, making a cracking noise. "Thanks for the sheets and pillow."

"I hope you didn't leave those things lying around your apartment." She continued to twirl and shuffle.

"The floorboards in the closet haven't been nailed down yet, so I lifted a couple up and tucked the stuff under there. I put the sleeve in there too."

"Well, I can't let you stay in our place. Mom's already suspicious that she hasn't met your mother yet. She thinks you might be a street hooligan. Up to no good."

Jake laughed, but Beth wasn't joking. "No. It's serious. I keep stalling her, but if she calls the cops or a truancy officer, you could get scooped up. We might have to find you a mom or she'll eventually stop letting us spend time together."

"Find me a mom? That's what I'm trying to do," Jake said. "*My* mom. Anyway, I don't plan to be here long enough to make it a problem."

Beth nodded but didn't say anything.

Jake was more nervous than he let on. He'd waved a quick goodnight to Beth's mom after they left the concert and had even pretended he could hear his own mother calling from the elevator. Luckily Beth's mom hadn't followed him over.

She had seemed nice and had called after him to "let us drop by and see you." But what if he got "scooped up" before he'd ever had a chance to figure out why he was here? What if she tried to visit his apartment?

Beth guessed his thoughts. "I told her I'm not sure what apartment you're in. That won't work for long, though."

"But what if she follows me or starts snooping around?"

Beth continued dancing. "Too busy. She works almost dawn to dusk."

"Doing what?"

She frowned. "Mostly cleaning houses for rich people. Amazing how messy people can be when they have a lot of stuff. She's always looking for something better."

Jake had a sudden vision of his own mom, searching for the same "better" thing. He wondered if she'd gotten her new job. Or was she now searching the city for her missing son? His stomach knotted.

Beth slowed and bowed to her broom dance partner. "Mom says I might have to quit school to join her if things don't get better soon."

"Quit school to work? You're just a kid. Isn't that illegal?"

She rolled her eyes. "You really are a rube. My mom's been cleaning sheets, floors, and dishes since she was way younger than I am. Dad vowed I wouldn't have to, but . . ." She suddenly concentrated very hard on her sweeping.

"What happened to your dad?"

77

Beth stopped sweeping but gripped the broom handle tight. "It's a long story, and a short one."

"Apparently I'm not going anywhere," Jake said. "But only if you want to talk about it."

She took a deep breath. "The short story is that he fought in the Great War and got sick and died."

Jake wasn't a hundred percent sure what she meant by "the Great War," but he didn't want to interrupt her.

"The longer story is this: I was just a little kid, but I still remember going to the train station with Mom to wave goodbye. He was wearing this green uniform, like the colour of muddy grass, but so was everyone else. I had trouble spotting him on the train. Every window seemed to be filled with men in green.

"Then, just as the train started to speed away, he saw me and waved. He looked so small as the train disappeared. There was a band playing songs about going 'over there' and how soon they'd all be coming home. He did come home, but when he did, he was so sick. He'd been gassed. It ruined his lungs. He never really recovered."

"I'm so sorry."

Beth wiped her eyes on her sleeve. "He and Mr. Williams had designed this place and built much of it before the war started. Father came back, and once he got out of hospital, he poured everything he had left into this work."

"He was an amazing artist," Jake said, and he meant it.

"Yes." She looked up at the vaulted ceiling, her eyes watering. "He was there, on some scaffolding, finishing carving the arches. Mr. Williams was in the balcony." She paused and breathed a deep sigh. "Father was taken with a coughing fit. He was climbing down the scaffolding when he blacked out. Mr. Williams had rushed to help and was there to catch him before he hit the floor. You noticed Mr. Williams's limp?"

Jake nodded. "Was that from catching your father?"

"Yes. Both legs broken. I think the limp reminds him every day of what happened."

"They must have been close."

"Like brothers. Father never woke up. They rushed him to hospital, but this time . . . he didn't come home."

They were silent for a while, the only sound the breeze gently rustling the curtains through the open windows.

Jake stared up at the distant ceiling. The arches were covered with carved heads and twisting vines even more ornate than the ones in the elevator. But one section, right where the two arches crossed, was still bare wood. The spot where Beth's father had stopped his work.

"Doesn't it make you sad to be in here?"

Beth nodded. "I refused to visit for a long time. Then one day, I was in the elevator with Mr. Williams and he got off at his office. The wall was open for some reason. I only caught a glimpse of the hall, but it just . . . made my heart swell. I know that sounds silly."

"Not at all," Jake said.

"That feeling stuck with me. A few days later, we were on the elevator again and I asked if I could join him. It was hard. But it was also as if I could see or maybe feel my father alive again, at least a little bit, in those rooms. In here, especially." She sighed. "My mom can't walk inside without breaking down. She says it reminds her of what she calls our 'flock of bad luck.' But I love seeing what he was able to make. The beauty he added to this world."

They stared at the ceiling in silence for a while.

"He used to tell me that it's not how long you live that matters. It's how *well* you live." She started sweeping again. "Of course, I intend to do both—live long and well."

Jake smiled at Beth's confidence, then stopped, worried he'd hurt her feelings.

But Beth laughed. "And who knows?" she said. "Maybe someday I'll do something to make the world more beautiful. Like me." She placed her hands under her chin, looked up, and smiled.

Jake felt his cheeks blush and quickly turned his attention back to sweeping.

"That's the long story," Beth said. "Now let's finish this work." She hummed to herself, dancing and sweeping at the same time.

Jake stopped and watched her for a minute, then went back to work. His mind swam with thoughts of his own mother, of Beth's family, and of how long he could pretend to be staying with her while actually crashing in what he hoped one day would be his apartment again.

Or would it ever become his apartment? What if he failed at whatever mission he'd been sent back to do?

A few nights, he'd waited until dark and snuck around the hallways, but he still hadn't uncovered any leads. The Regency was just the Regency, only younger.

He'd lain awake for hours, running through what had happened and what it could all mean.

If he'd gone backward in time, he must be able to go forward again. He wasn't even sure why he believed this, except that the alternative—that this was some random mistake—was too frightening to consider.

The day the Regency is slated for demolition, I go back and meet the man who designed it?

There had to be a reason.

He looked over at his new friend, sweeping and singing. Maybe he was here to help Beth somehow? He'd only known her for a day, and she was the least "I need help" person he'd ever met. He couldn't bring her father back. What could he do? What was he supposed to do?

The panels of the balcony slid apart, and Williams appeared at the railing.

"How goes the work?" he called.

"Great," Beth replied. "Almost done."

"Can I ask you two to run an errand for me after lunch? I just need a package delivered to the pharmacy."

Even on a normal day, the thought of going outside to deliver mail or run errands for Danny made Jake nervous. He'd always preferred inside to out, and the neighbourhood around the Regency, like the building itself, was run-down and more than a little sketchy.

So that gnawed at him. But there was something else. Having decided his reason for being here had something to do with the Regency, he was now nervous about leaving it. He felt anchored to the building somehow. He was suddenly struck by how weird that was. A building he couldn't wait to leave in the future was now the only place he wanted to be in the past.

"Hey, Jake," Beth said, snapping her fingers in front of his face. "You in?"

"Um, yeah. Sure."

Williams clapped his hands. "Great! And there's an extra quarter in it for each of you, just to recompense you for the added time." He closed the panels.

"A quarter!" Beth said with a huge grin. "What luck!"

Jake was shocked. "Seriously? A quarter? That's, like, noth-ing. How am I going to buy food?"

"Do you have any idea what you can buy with a quarter?"

Jake thought for a second. "Actually, no."

Beth shook her head sadly. "Well, we'll have to fix that."

CHAPTER THIRTEEN

As he and Beth stood on the marble floor of the front hallway, shiny quarters clutched in their hands, Jake began to rattle off excuses to skip this adventure.

"I'm not dressed right. Also, I have a cold. And what happens if I get run over by some rampaging horse?"

"Or if I push you in front of one for being such a stick-in-the-mud?" Beth said.

"Seriously! My mom will never know where I've gone. The Regency will be torn down. I'll never even know what I'm supposed to be doing here. Maybe you should go alone. I'll stay here."

Beth, of course, was having none of this. "What a Mrs. Grundy you are," she said.

"Who?"

"It means you're a no-good chicken. I'll be with you the whole time. And I have no plans—so far—to push you in front of anything. Well, except for a surprise taste of luxury. You're wearing my dad's old shoes and hat, so you even look sort of less weird than usual. *Acting* less weird is another matter. Now, move!"

She grabbed Jake by the arm and pushed open the doors.

He was instantly struck by the noise and the smell. It didn't smell worse than the city in his day, just different. There was less car exhaust but more of some smoky, stinky, grassy odour.

"What is that?" he asked.

"Horse manure." Beth pointed to what looked like a pile of fuzzy greenish-brown meatballs in the middle of the street.

"And they just *leave* that there?"

"There are street cleaners. Like that guy."

A few feet away, a man dressed in white and holding a broom walked alongside a horse cart that looked like a large garbage can on wheels. The man was sweeping up the dirt and manure.

"They collect it and sell it as fertilizer. Or dump it somewhere else."

Just as the man threw the poop from the street into the cart, his own horse pooped on the street.

"It's a make-work project apparently," Beth said.

Jake was going to make a joke about how much dirtier the streets were in the past, but he stopped. There were no used coffee cups, candy wrappers, or plastic bags lying around. And it wasn't that the streets were empty. The sidewalks were packed with people laughing, chatting, window shopping.

"Let's get moving," Beth said. She took Jake's hand in hers, and they marched down the busy sidewalk.

Signs in the windows read . . .

RCA VICTOR: The best wireless!
$65 will put a top-notch radio in your home, now!

Cash and carry: We sell for less!
Bread and jams as good as Mom makes!

Beth scoffed at that last one.

In Jake's day, there were only a few corner stores, some pawnshops, and a handful of businesses that sold things he probably didn't want to know about. Most of the shops that looked so clean and new in Beth's time would turn into empty storefronts with For Lease signs in the windows in Jake's. At least, the windows that weren't boarded up or broken.

"So where are we heading?" Jake asked.

"To see your pal Danny."

"Really?!"

"Just follow me."

They navigated through the throng and stopped in front of a huge glass window with "Figueredo's" painted on it in ornate gold letters.

Jake pointed at the sign on the door. "This says it's a drugstore."

"No kidding. Where do *you* get ice cream and soda?"

"Um, not at the same place I buy my toilet paper."

"Oh boy. C'mon, rube." She led him inside.

A tiny bell rang as Beth steered Jake into a brightly lit room. Tables with chrome tabletops and red leather seats lined one side wall below a huge window.

To their right, a glass case displayed shelves stacked with brightly coloured candies, tarts, and other sweets. Jake felt his stomach rumble and, salivating, tried to get a closer look.

But Beth grabbed him by the shoulder. "Nuh-uh. That's a clever distraction. The real treasure is always hidden at the back of the pirate's cave."

She pointed at a high counter that reminded Jake of the marble kitchen island he'd had in his old house. Dozens of bottles filled with brightly coloured liquids sat under a large mirror.

A man was adjusting the silvery knobs on a large metal box. There were signs on the counter for drinks Jake didn't recognize—Dr. Nut, Beppo—and others he did—Coca-Cola, Dr. Pepper, Canada Dry.

"Those are this old?" Jake pointed at the signs.

"You still have colas where you come from?" Beth pretended to be shocked. "I can't wait for the future to arrive!"

"Ha-ha. Some of them are still around. My mom drinks a lot of Canada Dry."

"I'm more of a Beppo fan myself."

"Never heard of it."

Beth shrugged. "We're here for better fare anyway."

She led Jake to the counter, and the man turned around.

Jake deflated a bit. Yes, the man had a name tag that read "Danny," but it wasn't *his* Danny.

"Well, if it isn't Miss Matthewson," said the man. "What's your poison?"

"I'll take chocolate."

"The regular. Very good. And you, young man?" He turned to Jake with a smile.

"Um, whatever she says is good, I guess."

"Ever had a malted, Jake?"

"I don't even know what that is."

Beth smiled and turned to Danny. "He'll have a malted with coconut."

"Excellent choice," said Danny. "You go find a seat and I'll start your orders lickety-split." He stood there for a second, smiling at Jake, then motioned his head toward the cash register.

"Your treat, Jake," Beth said with a grin. She walked to a window at the back of the store and slid Williams's package into a slot labelled Deliveries.

Jake held out his quarter. "I'm afraid this is all I have."

Danny smiled. "Well, I'll see if I can make change."

"Change?" Jake looked back at Beth.

She pointed to a painted metal sign over the mirror.

Malted 10¢
Ice cream shake 10¢

Danny handed Jake a nickel back.

"Um, you keep the change," Jake said.

"Well, thanks, big spender!" Danny smiled. Then he reached over and pulled four licorice sticks from a glass jar, wrapped them in paper, and handed them to Jake. "Two shoelaces for you and two for your friend. On the house."

Jake beamed. He beamed even more after Danny handed him a tin cup filled with a delicious brown ice cream concoction. Another glass contained some kind of milky liquid.

"Thanks!" He took his seat across from Beth.

"This is a malted? Is it any good?"

"You'll see."

Jake sipped his malted with coconut and his eyes bulged. "This is amazing! It's like my tongue is being tickled by vanilla."

"See? You should always listen to me. I'm a genius."

"So, genius," Jake said between sips, "if you're so smart, tell me—why am I here?"

"This is where my dad and Mr. Williams used to come and talk about their plans for the Regency." She took a spoonful of her ice cream. "They'd also bring me here for treats and stuff."

"Um, okay. I meant, why am I *here*? In your time?"

Beth cocked her head.

Jake sighed. "Humour me, okay?"

"Fine. I figured this might be a good place to put our two heads together and think of some possible answers." Beth picked up one of the licorice strings and began chewing meditatively. "So let's play a game," she said. "Let's play 'Jake isn't making stuff up.'"

"I'm not."

"You say you're from the Regency, but in the future."

"Yes."

"And the Regency is in trouble?"

"Yes."

"And what was the last thing that happened before you got . . . sent back in time?" She downed the last of her ice cream, licked the inside of the bowl, and leaned back with a satisfied smile.

"Well, a lot, actually. Mom was on her way to a job interview. My friends at the Regency were doing okay, I think."

"Friends. Mom. Good. Go on."

"And *my* Danny, the superintendent, had just showed me a letter from the city saying that the Regency was going to be demolished. He said that Mr. Williams had left some money for the place, but it had run out. Then I got a call from apartment 713, unlocked the door, and met you. My lucky day, I guess."

Beth didn't react. She was chewing on the licorice and staring at something out the window. "Well," she said, "it seems obvious that you've got to do something *now* that helps save the Regency *then* . . . in the future."

"Like what?"

"Get a job and save up money, maybe?"

Jake looked at the almost empty malted glass. "I just blew my first whopping twenty-five-cent bonus."

Beth sighed. "I'm no banking whiz, but I'm pretty sure that a few dollars a week isn't going to add up to enough to save a whole building." She pushed her nose against the window, peering into the distance. Jake, facing the other way, turned and tried to see what she was looking at, but he couldn't see anything out of the ordinary.

"I don't plan to be here longer than a week, if I can help it."

Beth took another bite of licorice. "My dad read me a book once about a guy who goes back in time."

"Seriously? Like a true story?"

"Hard to say with books. He goes back to the Dark Ages or something. Then he uses modern technology, like electricity and guns and stuff, to beat an army of people with swords. Can you make one of those fancy radio show recording thingies? We could sell those."

"Um, no. Not really."

"The guy also knows there was a solar eclipse on this one day and predicts it, so they think he's a wizard or something. Do you know anything that happens in the past like that? Maybe something you can make a lot of money from?"

89

"Like what?"

"You know, the winner of a horse race? Or some sporting event you can bet on?"

"Um, not really. History was never really my thing at school. I tend to google stuff."

Beth's eyebrows raised high. "That word again."

"It means I look things up in a kind of online library."

"Like books hanging on a laundry line? Did they get wet?"

"Um." His mind felt fuzzy. How to explain? "It's like there's a really super big room with all sorts of books in it. Books on everything."

"Yeah. Sounds like a library. I love libraries."

"Cool. But the books in this library aren't real. And the room isn't real either. You click on the book."

"Click?"

"With your finger. Or a mouse."

"A MOUSE?"

"Not a real mouse. Look, it doesn't matter. You still read the book, but on a screen."

"A movie screen?"

"Sort of. But not really. It's more like a small screen that sits on your lap or on top of your table, or even in your hand."

"Like a book?"

"Yeah, but it's *all* the books, right there in front of you."

"Still sounds like a book. I think I'd rather read the book."

Jake banged his forehead on the tabletop.

They sat in silence for a bit while he racked his brain for anything that might be useful. He knew there was a big war on the way in a few years. But the specifics escaped him. Sports? He lifted his head. "Hmmm. I do know some baseball stuff."

"Such as?"

"The New York Yankees are really good right now."

"Anyone with a brain knows that. Ruth and Gehrig are amaz-ing. Throw in Lazzeri and Pennock, and they are unbeatable."

"Wait, YOU like baseball?"

Beth cocked her head and stared back at Jake. "Who doesn't, brainless?" She stood up. "Speaking of which, it's time to go."

"Where? We haven't figured anything out yet."

"My amazing brain needs a distraction. I spotted something perfect out the window. Follow me."

"Um, okay."

"Bye, Mr. Figueredo," Beth called as she marched across the floor and out the front door. Jake ran to keep up.

CHAPTER FOURTEEN

As they hurried back down the sidewalk, Jake stared up at the Regency, the only tall building for blocks. It was almost sparkling, as if the stone had just gone up as he and Beth enjoyed their ice cream.

It was a marvel.

Jake realized with a jolt that this was his first real look at the Regency from the outside. Not just today, in Beth's time, but even in his own. As Danny had said, Jake spent a lot of time looking at his shoes. And the few times he'd looked up when he was on his errands, it was obscured by other tall buildings and he'd caught only glimpses of it.

Now, though, only the street and three empty lots surrounded it.

Jake couldn't take his eyes off the ornate decorations. For the first time, he saw how amazing the building *looked*.

Delicately carved stone angels held up the building's top four corners. Polished copper eaves and downspouts shone like sunlight. A band of granite ran around the edge of the building, and there was a message carved into the stone: "A home is a place with heart. A heart makes a place a home. This is my home. You are always welcome here."

"The thing Danny told me about," Jake said.

"The what?" Beth turned and looked at him.

Jake pointed at the top of the building. "The stuff about this being a home."

"Oh yeah." Beth nodded. "I thought you were pointing at the lightning rods."

"Lightning rods?"

"The next time we have a thunderstorm, you gotta see it. Mr. Williams made the four corners of the building out of huge steel beams. They go way up and way down. And when lightning hits—wow! It's like electric candy floss dancing down the sides of the building."

"Really?"

"People stop and watch. It's kinda magical. I'll show you the next time we have a storm roll in. Now follow me," she said, marching away again.

Jake hesitated. He looked more closely at the inscription. The angels he could see were using only one hand to hold up a corner. With the other, each angel was pointing at . . . something. He shielded his eyes from the blazing sun. It was hard to tell exactly *what* they were pointing at. It seemed to be the inscription?

"Move it, slowpoke!" Beth yelled back over her shoulder.

Jake moved it.

They were heading for the dirt field that sat right behind the Regency. A group of about twenty kids had gathered in a tight circle. What they were surrounding was impossible to tell.

A kid on the outside of the circle saw them approaching.

93

"I'll be bumped! If it isn't Beth the Bloomer!" he yelled.

"The very same. What's up, kiddo? A game?"

"Even better! LOOK!" The boy stepped aside, revealing three men. Two were kneeling on the ground, signing baseballs, mitts, and everything from sticks to scraps of newspaper. The other was Williams, and he had his hand on the shoulder of the thinner of the two. They were laughing and telling jokes.

"I thought I smelled a baseball game," Beth said to Jake.

"Jake! Beth!" Williams said. "Meet my friends George and James."

"I think you mean the Babe and Cool Papa," Beth said. "Gentlemen, it is an honour to meet you."

"Thanks, kid," said Cool Papa Bell. He bowed low, taking off his wide-brimmed hat.

"Want us to sign a baseball?" asked Babe Ruth in a gravelly voice.

"Sure. If I can then use it to strike you both out on three pitches."

Babe Ruth let out a huge guffaw. "I like this kid! She's got spunk!"

Cool Papa Bell laughed too. "I bet I can run faster than your fastball, kid."

"Only one way to find out," Beth said. She reached down and picked up a baseball and began tossing it up and down in her left hand.

Jake was too shocked to speak. He'd only ever seen pictures of two of the greatest to play the game. And his new friend was trash-talking them? Maybe he hadn't gone back in time but to some strange alternative universe? He stood rooted to the spot, his mouth agape.

Williams assumed Jake was confused about how they all knew each other. "The Babe and Papa are staying at the Regency tonight," he explained.

"Okay." Jake seemed to be talking in slow motion.

"I played some semipro ball a few years back," Williams continued. "We all met on a barnstorming junket. I owe these two my career."

"Yup, his career in architecture," Cool Papa Bell said, laughing and continuing to sign souvenirs. "Did him a favour by showing him how bad he was at baseball."

Ruth reached out his enormous arms and gave Williams a hug, shaking him like a doll. "He had a cannon for an arm," Ruth said. "But a batting eye like . . . well, an architect."

Williams let out a belly laugh. "Can't argue with the truth," he said. "But we stayed in touch."

Bell nodded. "The Regency is a beautiful place to crash for a spell."

"Or to hide from the press," said the Babe.

"Always welcome." Williams patted his friend's shoulder. "They're playing an exhibition game tomorrow afternoon, if you want to watch."

"Game." Jake nodded slowly. "Wait?! With Babe Ruth . . . and Cool Papa Bell?" His head was spinning. "But isn't the season still going on?"

Bell snorted. "The Babe here gets an actual salary. Me? I'm not allowed in the so-called major leagues, so most of my money comes from paid exhibition games. I play those whenever I can."

"Extra cash never hurts. And I've got some time between games with the Yankees. I'll wear a beard and use a fake name

in case there are spies in the crowd. The fans eat that stuff up."
The Babe winked.

"Enough chatter," Beth said. "We playing some ball or not?"

The two men exchanged glances and smiles. Then the Babe
began to take off his jacket. "Sandlot ball. Just like when I was a
kid in the orphanage."

"You were in an orphanage?" Jake asked.

"We all got rough stuff in our past," Ruth said. "That's why
the world needs big-hearted folks like this fella." He jerked a
thumb toward Williams. "He doesn't judge people."

Cool Papa nodded. "Just helps 'em."

Beth marched to a spot in the middle of the field and kicked
a line into the gravel and dirt with the back of her heel. "This is
the rubber," she said.

Cool Papa Bell estimated where the batter should stand and
dropped his hat on the ground to mark the spot. "Home plate."

The other kids clamoured to set up bases with whatever
scraps of wood or cardboard they could rummage.

Beth pointed to the nearby sidewalk and then the field.
"Two teams. Half the kids play now, half after five runs. Then we
switch batters and fielders."

Jake watched in awe as the others obeyed, dividing them-
selves up without arguing. Who was this Beth kid?

The Babe set himself up behind the catcher. "I'll umpire for
your team, Papa. Then we'll switch?"

"Works for me," Bell said. And he settled himself into the
imaginary batter's box. "All right, Beth the Bloomer. Let's see
what you got."

"You won't be able to see it at all." Beth spat onto the
ground and wound up for the first pitch. She was a natural. She

sailed the first pitch in so hard that the catcher shook his hand in pain.

"STEE-RIKE ONE!" called the Babe.

Bell whistled. "Sign her UP."

Beth held her glove in front of her face. She tried not to smile, and failed. She actually looked over at Jake and winked.

On the next pitch, Bell started to swing for what he thought was a fastball, but he missed when Beth dropped a curveball right at his knees.

"STRIKE TWOO!" bellowed the Babe with a laugh that came straight from his belly.

"How did a kid learn to toss a hook like THAT?" Cool Papa Bell chuckled again. But his smile vanished and his eyes narrowed as he settled in for the third pitch . . .

Which ended up inside apartment 415 of the Regency.

Bell had hit the ball perfectly, launching a graceful arc into the blue sky and through the window with a crash.

Beth watched the home run in awe.

"You got talent. Keep it up, kid," Bell called to her as he jogged around the bases. "But never throw curves back to back, especially on an 0–2 count when I gotta swing."

Beth smiled. "Maybe I'll just plug you with a fastball next time."

A woman's head emerged from the window. "YOU ROTTEN KIDS—" Then she spied Williams in the midst of the crowd and stopped.

Williams cupped his hands around his mouth. "It's okay, Mrs. Ricci. I'll send up the glass repair." Then he pointed at Jake and Beth. "And my cleanup crew as soon as the game is over."

Mrs. Ricci nodded and disappeared back into her apartment.

Jake watched her go, then kept his eyes on the building. A large fluffy white cloud had moved in front of the sun, casting the Regency in a silvery shadow. The two angels here at the back corners of the building were also pointing. But at what?

Jake was distracted by another loud crack as Ruth came to the plate and launched Beth's fastball dangerously close to another window. It banged off the brick and bounced on the ground right back to the outfield.

"Lucky swing," Beth said.

The Babe laughed so hard he had to stop running the bases and bend over to catch his breath.

"Okay, time to change things up!" Beth called a few minutes later. She signalled for the players to switch, which was met with a groan from the kids on the field and a cheer from the new players.

Jake didn't budge.

Beth ran over, out of breath. Her hands, face, and dress were covered in dust, but she was smiling from ear to ear.

"You're not heading out there? I thought you said you liked baseball."

"Well, I do. But I'm not really a play—" Jake never got to finish the sentence as Beth grabbed him and dragged him into left field.

"Who's the new kid?" yelled the centre fielder.

"Drip from the future," Beth called. The centre fielder did a double take but then shook his head and went back to watching the action.

Beth picked up a glove from the field and handed it to Jake. It was nothing like the gloves he was used to. This one was barely padded, with leather so worn and rubbed with oil that it looked black.

"Seriously?" he said. "I've seen mittens with more protection." He wondered how many fingers he'd break if he *did* catch a baseball.

"Now just stand here, you sensitive bunny, and watch for a little white ball to appear in the big blue thing up there," Beth said.

"Ha-ha. I'm not totally useless," Jake said.

"Fooled me," Beth called back as she skipped over to stand next to Williams.

Jake looked around. There were dozens of kids, all smiling, laughing, and watching as a new pitcher, a gangly kid with holes in the knees of his pants, began spinning balls toward the plate. Kid after kid struck out or at best tapped the ball weakly to the infield.

"C'mon, Ace," yelled the centre fielder. "We're getting bored out here! Let 'em hit!"

On cue, the Babe came up and whacked a low screwball high into the air. Jake watched it rise higher and higher, like a bird. It seemed to disappear into the sky. It reminded him of the arches in the Great Hall. Soaring. Graceful.

Then it fell. And Jake realized with a panicked jolt that it was falling straight toward him. Everything that had seemed to be happening in slow motion was now in incredibly fast motion.

First, the sun emerged from behind the clouds, making him wince. He blinked and lost the ball. Where was it? His eyes darted around, the panic rising.

There! It seemed to pick up speed as Jake made lazy circles underneath, trying to figure out exactly where he needed to be to catch it. This wasn't like the video games he'd played in his room. What if he tripped? Or dropped the ball?

Voices came at him from all sides.

"There, there!!! LOOK UP!"

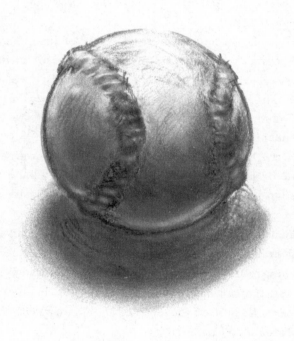

"Get your glove up!" The centre fielder.

"Eyes open!" Williams.

"Don't drop it, you palooka!" That was from Beth, of course.

Suddenly the ball seemed to come at him as fast as a bullet. He leapt sideways, where he hoped the ball was about to land, and tripped over his too-big shoes. As he fell, he thrust out his arm blindly.

Eyes closed, he felt the ball smack into his mitt just as his face whacked into a pile of grit, dirt, and pebbles.

There was a moment of silence and then cheering. But from which team? Oh no, he'd dropped the ball. The Babe was probably running the bases for an in-the-park homer.

He felt a shadow pass over his face, and he opened his eyes.

"Nice grab," Beth said, leaning over him.

Jake looked. The ball was firmly embedded in the webbing of the glove. His hand was throbbing.

She smiled. "You looked like a duck trying to catch a mosquito."

Cool Papa joined her. "Wasn't pretty, but it got the job done."

Then the Babe came over, jacket draped over his shoulder. "Nice one, kid. I think that ends the game on a high note. Me and Cool Papa should get something to eat." He patted his stomach. "But let us sign that ball before we head out."

"Really?" Jake asked, awed.

"Of course!" Ruth pulled a pen out of his pocket.

Jake handed him the ball.

"What's yer name, kid?" the two men asked.

Jake was about to tell them but stopped. "Can you sign it to Gus?"

CHAPTER FIFTEEN

I thought your name was Jake!" Beth was sweeping broken glass from Mrs. Rizzo's floor into a metal dustpan that Jake was holding.

"Gus is a guy I know."

"Does he live here?"

Jake nodded. "Apartment 804."

"Where the Katzes live now?"

"I guess so." Jake had spent a few more early mornings wandering the hallways, opening garbage chutes and knocking on the doors where his clients lived, or would someday. He'd gotten a few annoyed looks, but he was still no closer to finding a way back home.

"And Gus likes baseball?"

Jake thought about this. It was clearly true—Gus had baseball on all the time, and it was the one thing Jake could get him to talk about. But it was also hard to say what quiet Gus "liked."

"Yeah, I think he does." Jake stopped sweeping. "Actually, I think it helps him."

"Helps him?"

"Yeah. Calms him down. He's got PTSD or something."

"PTSD?"

"I'm not really sure what it stands for. The words 'trauma' and 'stress' are in there, I think. It just means that he lived through some awful stuff and it's made him . . . sad. Scared. I saw this tattoo on his forearm once. Two eagles and crossed swords. I think he was a soldier."

Beth had said nothing. Jake looked up. She was standing as still as a statue.

"What's wrong?"

"Your friend has shell shock."

"Shell shock?"

Beth nodded. "Remember I said there was a short and a long story about my dad?"

"Yeah."

"The long story is actually longer than what I told you before. He didn't come back to the Regency right away. My dad came home from the war and didn't talk for months. They sent him to a kind of recovery home. But he stayed in his bed and stared up at the ceiling. I visited him every day and read to him—his favourite book, *Treasure Island*, over and over. But he just kept staring."

"That sucks."

Beth took a few deep breaths before continuing. Her voice was soft, almost a whisper. "Finally, one day he turned to me and said my name. That was it. My name. Like he'd just noticed at that moment that I was there. I was too shocked to say anything. I just hugged him."

She sniffed and gave a small cough. "The next day, he told his doctors he was ready to go home. He said he had work to do.

They released him a few days after that. But even though he tried to act like nothing had changed, he wasn't really the same. At least not all the time. He never told us what had happened to him, but I'd see his hands start shaking. He'd lock himself away in the bedroom. I'd hear him coughing, talking to himself."

Jake got up and put a hand on her shoulder. "I'm so sorry. That must have been awful."

Beth wiped her eyes on her sleeve. "And my dad had a similar tattoo. Maybe he and Gus fought with the same unit?"

"I don't think Gus is that old."

Beth whacked him across the leg with the broom. "I didn't mean they fought together, you sap! It's just another weird connection. Another sign you're maybe not completely loony. There are some strange coincidences and connections between your time and this one."

Jake gave Beth a hug.

Beth seemed shocked at first, then she hugged Jake back. "What's this for?" she asked.

Jake took a step back. "Because that sounded like it was tough to talk about."

Beth nodded. "Yeah. Mom never really wants to talk. Thanks for listening. You're a good listener, Jake."

"And I also hugged you because that was the first time you *almost* admitted you believe me."

She smiled. "Almost."

They were interrupted by Williams coming through the door with a large wooden box. "I'm here, Mrs. Ricci. I trust my cleanup crew has been behaving?"

"*Si, si.* Yes," Mrs. Ricci called from the kitchen.

Beth turned away and wiped her nose on her sleeve.

Williams paused when he saw her, but only for a second. Then he walked over to the broken window.

"Looks ready," he said. He pulled two wooden tabs out of the top of the broken frame and it came loose. He took it out and set it aside, then opened the wooden box with a small pry bar.

"Is the new glass in there?" Jake asked.

"Not exactly."

Williams pulled out a brand-new frame, brushing off some loose pieces of straw packaging. He slipped the frame into the window casing and, once it was firmly in place, snapped the wooden tabs back in.

"One of my better ideas, actually. Everything in every apartment is made to a standard size, and I have a basement filled with replacements. Just pop out the old part and snap the new one in place. Ta-da!"

Jake made a mental note to look in the labyrinthine basement for a replacement window for his leaky one as soon as he got back home. If he ever got back home. He shivered at the thought.

"Now, since you two have finished cleaning up in here, I have a special treat for you. Oh! First, your wages."

He pulled out a worn leather wallet and handed Jake and Beth two crisp two-dollar bills each.

Thanks to the ice cream adventure, Jake knew this was not bad for a day's work—especially one that included a break for a baseball game *and* a signed baseball.

"Thanks!" he said.

"So what's the treat?" Beth asked. "Jake here is partial to malteds."

Williams shook his head. "This is even better than a malted.

Got something planned in the hall tonight, and I need a little help setting up."

Jake looked down at the bills in his hand. Beth had said she was no math whiz, but she was right that there was zero chance working for 1920s wages was going to allow him to save anything.

But Beth spoke first. "Well, for an extra twenty-five cents, you can count me in."

Williams let out a howl and shook his head. "You are incorrigible. But deal."

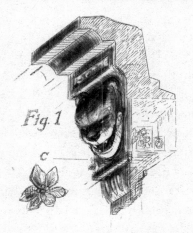

Fig. 1

c

CHAPTER SIXTEEN

The treat turned out to be a movie, but Williams refused to say which one. He just told the kids they'd "get a kick" out of it. And if they showed up early, he said, he'd pay their bonus and let them watch the film from his secret balcony.

"But first, eat some dinner. I'll see you down here at seven o'clock."

Dinner, for Jake, was another smuggled sandwich from Beth with some fruit he'd bought at the grocery across the street. He ate it all while sitting cross-legged on the floor of apartment 901.

He washed himself off in the kitchen sink. The bathtub and shower attachment hadn't been hooked up yet. Luckily, the toilet was operational. Each time Jake used it, he looked askance at the toilet paper roll Beth had given him—which she'd told him was "mostly splinter-free." What would "splinter-*full*" toilet paper feel like? He didn't want to know.

There was a knock on the doorjamb of the apartment. The door itself was still missing.

"Be right there!"

He finished dressing—in more of Beth's dad's ill-fitting clothes—and walked to the door.

Beth was waiting for him. She was looking down the hallway to her right, making sure the coast was clear. Her curly hair was tied in a green ribbon, and her jaw, as always, jutted out slightly, as if she was getting ready to spit out an acerbic remark or a joke.

She was the most amazing person Jake had ever met, and he wasn't even sure she was real.

She noticed him staring. "What are you gawking at?"

"Just keeping quiet in case there's someone out there," Jake lied.

"Well, now I finally know how to shut you up."

"Wait—you think I talk too much?" Jake stood in the doorway, shuffling his feet. "Beth, I'm not lying about where I come from, you know. And I want to get back. My mom is . . . she's already going through a lot."

Beth nodded. "Okay."

"But I do like spending time with you. You're . . ."

"Going to help you figure this out, Jake."

Jake beamed.

She grabbed his hand. "Now let's go. Lickety-split, we gotta get to work."

The ballroom was equipped with a movie screen, but it required some effort to set up. Jake and Beth worked a series of pulleys behind the stage, and the screen lowered from a gap between the wall and the ceiling. Two angels flanked the opening, as if they were unrolling the screen.

"Seriously, this place just never stops impressing me," Jake said.

Beth threw him some ropes to anchor the bottom of the screen to the stage. "It's nice to see Mr. Williams excited about things again. Like the concert and this movie."

"Isn't he always excited by the Regency?"

Beth tied off one of the ropes. "Ever since my father died, he's lost some—a lot—of his energy. That's why work on the ninth floor stopped. He and Dad had all these plans. It was going to be the penthouse floor. Not bigger rooms but fancier, with nicer finishes and paintings on the walls. There were rough drawings my dad made, but after he died, we couldn't find them."

"That's too bad." Jake thought of how drab and basic his room was, even in his own time.

"Yeah, it is." She clapped the dust off her hands. "All right, let's get the chairs set up."

As they laid out the rows of folding chairs, Jake kept steal-ing looks at the ceiling and the angels who were "holding" the screen. "It's cool the way they trick you into thinking the angels are doing that. And their wings hide the slot in the ceiling where the screen comes from."

"Dad and Mr. Williams always said that every decorative element also had to have a practical purpose."

"Every one?"

"Yes. Think about the garbage chute."

"The hippo's mouth." Jake nodded. "And the way the bear's paw opens the wall to reveal the balcony."

"Yup."

They continued unfolding and positioning the chairs. At one point, Beth held a chair in one hand and pointed with the other.

"Let's start the last row here," she said.

Jake laughed.

"What?"

"Well, since we've been talking about angels, you just looked a bit like the ones on the outside of the building."

Beth flapped her arms like wings. "I have been described as angelic."

"I doubt that."

"Ha-ha."

"I meant that you were pointing like the angels on the outside of the building. They're decorative but also practical."

"Because they're holding up the building?"

"No. I mean, yes. But I think they're doing something else too."

"The pointing, you mean?"

"Yeah. That can't be an accident." Jake paused. He'd been thinking about the angels ever since he'd seen them, and Beth's comment about how all the decorations did two jobs got his brain working again. "I have a theory about them. It might be a bit weird."

"I can guarantee that if it comes from your brain, it'll be weird."

"What an angelic thing to say," he joked. "I just mean that I think what they are pointing at might be important."

Beth unfolded and placed another chair. "What are they pointing at?"

"I walked around the building after our baseball game to be sure. And I think they're pointing at words."

"Words?"

"Yup. On the inscription. Two of them are pointing at the word 'home' in the phrases 'A home is a place with heart' and 'A

heart makes a place a home.' The
third one is pointing at the word
'heart.'"

"And the fourth one?"

"It's pointing at the
word 'here' in 'You are
always welcome here.' So
'heart,' two 'homes,' and
a 'here.' I wonder if that
means anything?"

"Besides the obvious?
Like this is a home, and home
is where your heart is?"

"Maybe. Look, I'm still
working this all out. But you said
your dad loved mysteries and puz-
zles, right?"

Beth nodded. "He was always hiding
stuff for Mr. Williams to figure out later. Like the
keys and the doors in the balcony room."

She stared at the ceiling, locking her eyes on the unfinished
section where her father had been forced to stop his work. "But
if the angels are pointing at something on the outside of the
building, what are we supposed to do? I don't think he'd have
wanted someone scaling the wall to take a look at a brick."

"Yeah, like Spider-Man."

"Mr. Sniderman? The guy who sells radios? He's ancient.
No way he's climbing anything higher than a chair. Even that
might kill him."

Jake made a mental note that Spider-Man had probably

not been created yet. "Never mind. Like I said, I'm still working it all out. It could mean nothing." He went back to lining up the chairs.

Beth did too, but Jake could see she was thinking.

They finished with the chairs just as Williams opened the doors. People began making their way inside.

"Nicely done," Williams said. "You are a fine pair of workers."

"We care about this place," Beth said.

Jake nodded.

Williams smiled a wistful smile. "Well, that means a lot. It truly does. Now, if you two would join me in the balcony, we can get the show started!"

Jake had never seen Beth look so excited. "I love films. Especially ones with pirates. Does this one have pirates, Mr. Williams?"

"Um, no. At least, I don't think so."

Williams slipped his key into the broken button for the third floor, and the elevator took them up to his private room. The architect motioned to the chairs nearest the railing, and Jake and Beth sat down. Beth was so fidgety she could barely sit still.

Williams shook the bear's paw, and the walls slid apart. He leaned over the railing and addressed the crowd below. "Good evening, everyone. Take your seats and we will get underway soon. Mr. Marx will be accompanying our film tonight."

"What does that mean?" Jake asked Beth.

"He plays the music."

"Music?"

"Yeah, for the movie. He's down there on the piano." Beth pointed to a man in a brown suit who was theatrically laying out sheet music on an upright piano.

"But if he's playing during the movie, how do you hear the actors talking?"

"Talking? You have some funny ideas, Jake."

Jake wasn't sure what that meant, but before he could ask, the lights went down and a silver beam shot out from somewhere just above the balcony.

The "Flying Ace": Part One appeared on the screen, shimmering white on a black background. Music from the piano mixed with excited chatter and a few cheers from the audience.

Jake leaned close to Beth. "Everything is black and white. What happened to the other colours?"

"What are you talking about? Be quiet and watch the picture."

Jake sat back in his chair. "I guess we're not watching Star Wars."

"SHHHHH." Beth socked him gently on the shoulder.

Jake stayed quiet and watched, confused. Not by the plot—that was simple enough. Someone had stolen a railroad's payroll and framed the man who ran the local station. He just happened to have a daughter the villain wanted to marry. There was a goofy cop, a dentist with sleeping gas, and a man with one leg who could race on a bicycle and had a gun hidden in his cane. A returning war hero, a flying ace who was also conveniently a railroad detective, shows up to help solve the crime.

Jake sat through the first ten minutes wondering if there was a problem with the film. The actors didn't talk. Well, they did, but you couldn't hear them. So you had to guess what they were saying. Every once in a while, the whole screen would be filled with words explaining who people were or what they were talking about, and some bits of actual dialogue, but that was it.

And it was all in a weird silvery, flickering monochrome.

Jake was used to full colour, loud explosions, actual talking. Then he looked over at Beth. He saw the look of wonder on her face, her unwavering smile illuminated by the light. She sat on the edge of her seat, her hands either clutching the velvet cushion or clasped together in front of her mouth. When things got tense, she actually bit down on her knuckle.

What was she seeing? What was Jake missing?

He turned back to the screen and tried to see it through her eyes. He heard Beth and the crowd boo when the villain knocked the hero to the ground and hiss when he kidnapped the daughter. They gasped when the plane carrying the villain and the daughter caught fire in midair.

Jake was soon gripping the edge of his chair like everyone else. He began to boo with the crowd. He laughed when the oafish cop tried to capture the hero's friend. He cheered when the hero saved the daughter with a stunt airplane trick and a rope ladder.

As the closing credits rolled, he turned to look at Beth again. And he smiled.

The house lights came up just then, and he quickly swivelled his head back, pretending to look at the credits on the screen.

"Oh, Mr. Williams, that was . . . WONDERFUL!" Beth said. She got up and gave him a huge hug.

"Yeah. Wow!" Jake said. "They could have used some CGI for the airplane fight scenes, maybe."

"Sea what?" Williams asked.

"Um. I meant, 'See? Gee, I really enjoyed it.'" Jake gave a thumbs-up.

"Sure," Williams said slowly. "Well, it's getting late. I'm glad you enjoyed the show."

"We'll be here bright and early to clean up," Jake said.

"Very good. I don't know what this place would do without the Bobbsey twins."

"The who?" Jake looked at Beth.

"You should read more. Maybe you can gluegoop it later."

"Ha-ha."

"I prefer *Anne of Green Gables* anyway." Beth turned back to Williams. "Thanks ever so much, Mr. Williams. Hey! Maybe I could be a pilot someday! Or a railroad detective. Or both!"

"See? Gee, I think that would be great!" Jake tried again.

Williams gave a kind smile, walked over to the balcony edge, and waved to the crowd. "Thanks for coming, everyone. We'll have another film next week. Harold Lloyd's latest."

There were cheers and clapping from below. Williams turned around and leaned back on the railing. He was looking down at the marble floor of the balcony, rubbing his chin in his fingers.

Beth was already in the elevator, holding the door for Jake. Jake was about to step inside when Williams called out to him.

"Jake, can you stay behind for a few minutes? I think we need to have a little chat."

Jake felt a nervous shiver as the elevator door closed on a worried-looking Beth.

CHAPTER SEVENTEEN

ave a seat, please," Williams said in a stern voice, still leaning against the balcony railing.

Jake sat. He could hear the audience filing out of the hall below. "Yes, sir?" He fidgeted in his chair.

"Jake, I know that you're concealing things from me."

Jake felt a bead of sweat trickle down his back. "Sorry?" he squeaked.

Williams rolled his hand in the air. "I don't mean you are stealing things—I have found you more than trustworthy on that account. I mean you have not been completely honest about who you are, where you come from."

Jake's heart began to pound. He immediately wanted to be almost anywhere else.

Williams began pacing back and forth. "I've been noticing strange things. The words you use. Some of the clothes you wear." He stopped pacing and looked right at Jake again. "You're not Beth's cousin, are you?"

Jake gripped the arms of the chair tightly. He had to push out his words. "No, sir. I'm not."

Williams rubbed at his leg, then slid a chair across from Jake and sat down. "And you're not from around here, are you?" His voice was now softer, kinder.

Jake wasn't sure how to answer that. "I'm originally from Maypole Woods," he said. He gulped. Did Maypole Woods even exist yet?

Williams considered this for a second, then pushed out his lips and nodded. "Farm kid. No city smarts. Like a lost puppy. That makes some sense."

Now Jake wasn't sure if Williams was kidding him or believed him. "Yeah. I've never been in a place like this before, for sure." He pointed to the ornate decorations and the gilded ceiling of the room and the Great Hall beyond. He marvelled again at how lifelike the figures in the vaulted ceiling appeared. "Mr. Williams, I love the Regency."

As soon as he'd said it out loud, he knew it was true.

Williams looked over his shoulder at the hall and then turned back to Jake. "I know you do. It means a lot to me as well. But I also know you've been sleeping on the floor in 901."

Jake's eyes quickly locked back onto Williams. *Oh no. Busted,* he thought.

"And you've started a nice little collection in there. A signed baseball. Mr. Armstrong's autograph. I make it my business to know what's going on in our home."

"I . . . I . . . I can explain."

Williams held up his hand to stop Jake. "I'm not judging. And you are not necessarily in any trouble." He took a deep breath. "People come to the Regency for many reasons. Now, the truth, please."

Jake took a deep breath. The truth. "I wasn't lying about my mom. She lost her job. Her partner left. It's been hard. She is looking for work, and I'm here on my own while she does that." It was all true, Jake thought, if slightly tweaked.

Williams nodded along. He spoke slowly. "I am not a man who kicks people in need out of their homes. And, Jake, this *is* your home."

Jake stared in shock as Williams pulled a key out of his pocket and handed it to him. "This is a key to the door for 901."

"Door?"

"I took the liberty of installing one when you were setting up the chairs. It was long overdue."

Jake couldn't believe his ears. "So you're working on the building again?"

"Yes. I haven't been myself in a while. But I think it's time I got back to work. And that means getting that ninth floor to resemble, at least somewhat, what Charles and I had envisioned."

Jake was in shock. "Um, I don't know what to say. This is . . . wow!"

"I know that Beth is taking care of you. You have a good head on your shoulders. More than that. I believe you have a good heart."

Jake thought of the inscription on the building. "A home is a place with a heart, right?"

"Yes." Williams smiled. "Yes, it is. And you promise that your mother is coming here?"

Jake nodded. "Not right away." *The understatement of, literally, the century,* he thought. "But yes."

"Then this is your home. And it will be her home when she arrives." Williams took a folded piece of paper out of his jacket and placed it on a side table with a golden fountain pen. "Just sign the lease. And an X is fine if you haven't learned to spell yet. I'll have your mother make this official when she gets here."

Jake stared at the lease and the key, then raised his head to look at Williams. "What about rent?"

"The deal is that you use your time here to expand and improve your life. You pay what you can—a little or plenty—and you pay it forward when you are able. For now, let's consider half your pay as a down payment. Deal?"

Jake looked back at the lease. Angels drawn in dark indigo lines surrounded the text. One pointed at the words "The Regency," written in flowing script along the top of the page.

"Angels. Home," Jake whispered. Then he grinned. "That's what the angels are pointing to on the outside."

Williams beamed. "You caught that?"

"The words from the inscription. Home. Heart. Here."

Williams sat back in his chair and smiled. "I had already come up with the words, and the idea to put them around the top of the Regency. Charles said that was because I was always putting the head before the heart." He chuckled. "So he said he was going to make sure the heart got some attention."

"By having the angels point at the words."

"Something only a person with an observant eye would catch."

"Thanks. So if the top of the building is the head . . ."

"We're sitting in the heart right now." Williams gestured upward.

"This room?"

Williams nodded. "It's the direct centre of the building. The heart of the Regency is here."

"The third floor?" Jake did some quick math in his head. Nine floors and a basement made ten. "Wouldn't the fifth floor be the halfway point?"

"Another hidden secret, invisible from the street. But if you know the true depth of the Regency—what's hidden underneath—you know where the centre is."

"Huh?" Jake said. "I'm not totally sure I get what you mean."

"It was another of Charles's wonderful ideas. Simple math he hid in the details when we drew up the blueprints."

Jake arched an eyebrow.

"Maybe it's easier if I show you." Williams pointed up and down from two imaginary corners. "If you draw a line from each corner of the roof to each opposite corner of the foundation, deep under the ground, they actually meet in the middle, out there." He motioned toward the Great Hall. "Charles was so clever and fun. God, I miss him." He turned away and stared over his shoulder at the darkening hall. But Jake could see the tears in his eyes.

"You loved him, didn't you?"

"More than anything." Williams bowed his head, and his shoulders sagged. "Sorry, Jake." He rubbed the space between his eyes with his fingers. "I miss him. He was an artist. He could have been famous. He *should* have been. If only he had lived a little bit longer."

"Beth said being here is like being with him."

Williams smiled. "I see so much of Charles in her. Spirit and talent." He sat forward. "And I think she's right. I distracted myself from my sorrow with shows, concerts, movies, and yet this hall still felt empty. But I've been seeing the Regency through different eyes these days."

"You needed glasses?"

Williams let out a loud laugh. "No! I mean your eyes—and Beth's. It's reminded me of what Charles and I wanted to build together. And I think it's time I finished what he and I started."

Williams stood slowly, favouring his right leg. He walked to the wall and ran his hands over the carved animals and delicate vines. He pushed the lion's nose, revealing the key. He held it in his hand and smiled, then carefully placed it back and closed the lion's jaw.

Then he pressed the button for the elevator. "I've kept you here long enough, Jake. Now go get some rest." He returned to his seat, leaning back in the chair heavily.

"I get why the Regency means so much to you." Jake paused, collecting his thoughts. Maybe this was the moment—the reason he was here. To share what he knew about the future. "And you're right that I haven't told you everything. There's more."

Williams leaned forward. "Meaning?"

"The Regency. It's in danger."

Williams raised an eyebrow. "Danger? Does some anarchist want to destroy this place?"

Jake shook his head. He needed to get this right, but he also needed Williams to believe him. "No. It's not like that. I mean that in the future, it's crumbling . . . I mean it will be. It *could* crumble. The city will demolish it."

Williams released a long slow breath and sat back. "Ah. That's all."

"That's all?"

"Alas, this prospect is not unexpected."

Jake was confused. "What about the carvings? The Great Hall? What about the people who live here? What about . . . ?" This wasn't the reaction he had expected.

"That's what buildings do, Jake. They are like us, constrained by an arc. By time. They—and we—age and decay. They—and we—die. But *how* do we live *while* we live? That's the important question."

"But if it starts to crumble, it can get fixed, right?"

Williams got up and walked over to the railing. He rapped his knuckles on the polished wood. "This beautiful ribbon of oak is solid. It keeps me from falling to the floor. But look closer. It is already scuffed, chipped, scratched. And it came from a tree that itself was once alive. Now changed from one state into another."

"So a building can . . . die?"

Williams leaned against the railing. "The mortar outside that holds the bricks together? Just days after it was applied, the wind was already carving out pockets of dust. The crisp edges on the carved stone are becoming softer, smoother every day. Even the beauty of the angels will be wiped away by time."

"But . . . but . . . this place is special. You just said you are going to start work on it again. You just said so!"

Williams took a deep breath and stroked his chin. "I am not wishing for the end of the Regency. Far from it. But if the idea behind the Regency's existence is *lost* in the desire to save some pretty bricks and stone . . . well, then the building is dead anyway."

"The Regency can't die! What am I doing here if that's going to happen anyway?"

Williams looked askance at Jake. "I'm not exactly sure what

you mean. Great cathedrals have fallen, never to rise again. Great castles have been stormed, reduced to rubble. Humble homes collapse. Their mud walls return to the earth. If the idea for that building is good and it survives, that's all that matters."

"But you've poured your heart and soul into this place."

"Yes. And all my money too. Charles did as well. But it was never to create a physical thing, no matter how beautiful. It was because of an idea. An idea Charles and I shared."

Jake had to close his eyes so he could concentrate on trying to understand what Williams was telling him. "So what is this idea?"

"Home."

"Home?"

"That everyone deserves a roof over their heads. Everyone. It doesn't matter where they come from, or what they look like, or whom they love. And not just any home but a good place, a fine place . . . a special place. A place they can always come back to. A place they will *want* to come back to."

Jake's cheeks burned. "But how can they come back to a place if it doesn't exist anymore?"

Williams tapped his fingers along the wood. "Should I stop my work? Is the Regency falling any time soon?"

"No."

"Then what I hope is that the people who live here before that time comes—who are helped by the opportunity to live here when the world has cast them aside, when they have no other place to go—I hope that they will always share the *idea*. Then they will build ten Regencys, a hundred. That will make a better world. A chain of hope. This Regency is just the first link—or if we let the idea fail, the only one . . . and the last."

Jake thought of the dying building he had left behind. The people who lived there were soon to be kicked out onto the street. Lily and Gus were never going to "pay it forward." They were going to be left behind. Somewhere the chain Williams was talking about had been broken. And Jake had no way of knowing when or why, or how to fix it.

"But how do you keep that idea going once *you're* gone?" Jake asked.

"You ask some tough questions, young man," Williams said. "And I don't have all the answers. But I'll make a deal with you: you keep asking them, and I'll keep *trying* to answer."

"Just promise me that you'll do your best to make sure the Regency can survive as long as possible."

Williams took a deep breath. "I didn't come from money, Jake. Before the war, I made some money by using this." He tapped his forehead. "I have a gift, so they say, for the stock market. I don't see that gift disappearing anytime soon. And so long as I am making money, the Regency will be well taken care of. Now, it's getting late and you should probably join Beth in the elevator."

"Beth?" Jake looked back and saw the open elevator door. At some point, it had returned. And for a split second before she tucked it away, Jake saw Beth's right shoe in the open doorway.

"Bobbsey twins indeed," Williams said with a smile. "Now, good night."

Jake stepped into the elevator and pushed the button for the seventh floor. He looked down at his friend and saw that she had been crying.

He sat down next to her as the elevator rose. She was trembling.

"How much did you hear?" Jake asked.

"Enough. Is it really that bad?"

"I told you that where I come from, the Regency is about to be demolished. I think I'm here to help save it."

"All my father's hard work? All the things he made, built? And Mr. Williams is just willing to let it all"—she waved her hands in the air—"fade away?"

"I'm not going to let that happen. Mr. Williams isn't going to let that happen. He heard my warning. He listened. You heard him."

"I heard him say that it didn't matter. That the Regency, like my father, is going to die anyway."

Jake hugged Beth. She continued to cry. "Beth, I promise you, with everything I've got, I will not let that happen."

"Swear?"

"Swear."

But Jake had no idea how he could keep that promise.

CHAPTER EIGHTEEN

The movie crowd is way messier than the concert crowd," Beth called out, sweeping up a pile of loose wrappers, peanut shells, and other junk.

Jake reached down and picked up some brightly coloured bits of paper. "Milk Duds. Baby Ruth. We still have those where I come from!" He picked up a red-and-white Baby Ruth. "Hey! This one isn't even opened."

"Well, time for a snack break!" Beth said. They sat down on the floor. Jake tore off the wrapper, snapped the bar in half, and handed Beth her share.

"Buried treasure," Beth said, popping the whole piece into her mouth.

"This tastes different," Jake said. "The chocolate is less sweet or something."

"Still good?"

"Heck yes." Jake let the last of the chocolate melt in his mouth before crunching the nuts. "And the peanuts are more peanutty."

"I'm not sure that's a word. Or maybe it is where you come from?"

"It is now. Peanutty. Peanutty."

Beth laughed and lay down on her back.

Jake joined her on the floor so that the tops of their heads were touching. The sunlight streamed in through the giant windows, making the ceiling glow.

"Wow," Jake said. "That is beautiful."

"I've always wondered what those angels were looking at," Beth said.

"The ones outside? Glad I could help."

"I'm talking about the ones in here."

She pointed over Jake's head toward the corners of the room. A column in each corner was topped with a knot of twisting vines, leaves, and flowers. But peeking out from each, almost completely hidden, were the torso and wings of an angel.

Each angel was looking up, with one hand touching its chest and the other raised. Each one was looking along the length of the arch above it. And each arch curved up until all four met in the middle of the ceiling, forming an X—at the exact spot where Beth's father had stopped working the day he'd died.

"You have got to be kidding me," Jake said. "It can't be." He stood up quickly, his eyes still locked on the X. He'd seen the cross before, but now his brain started to piece together everything he'd learned about the Regency.

"What?" Beth stood up next to him.

"You said *Treasure Island* was the book you read to your dad in the hospital?"

"About a hundred times. His favourite when he was a kid. I love it too. You know that. It's got pirates!"

Jake nodded. "And your dad knew you knew that too. Which is why he left you a clue from the book so you could find . . . well, I'm not sure what, but something."

"What do you mean?"

"Look." Jake traced his finger in the air, along the length of each arch.

Beth's eyes grew wide. "An X marks the spot."

"The angels outside tell you to look for the heart. I think that's why they also point at the word 'here.' Mr. Williams told me the Great Hall—here—is the heart of the building."

"And the angels in here point to that X as the heart of the room?"

"That's the message your dad wanted you to discover."

Beth stood still for a few seconds, thinking, then she beamed. "If I could, I'd fly up there right now."

"Or maybe we can ask Mr. Sniderman to climb?"

She responded by socking Jake's arm.

"Ouch! Are there any ladders around here that would reach?"

Beth stared back up at the X. "My dad used special scaffolding, not a ladder."

"Well, that isn't the bee's knees."

Beth chuckled.

"What's so funny?"

"You used one of my phrases. Sort of. You don't say something *isn't* the bee's knees. You can just say it's too bad."

"Applesauce."

"Ha! You're really starting to fit in around here, Jake."

He blushed, then felt a pang of guilt as he remembered his mom. She was probably frantically searching for him. Or maybe she'd given up. He'd been gone for more than a week. A *week*. He glared at the *X*, and it stared down at him.

Beth and Williams had said her father had "buried a treasure," but they'd never been able to find it. Now they had a lead, a solid idea of where the treasure might be hidden.

Was it real treasure? Money? Enough to save the Regency? Was *that* why he'd been yanked back in time? If he was right, would that reveal some way for him to get home? It was the closest he felt to an answer since he'd walked into apartment 713.

Somehow, he needed to get up there.

"The exact spot where he stopped," Beth said in an awed whisper. "I feel a little like one of those shipwrecked pirates from the *Walrus*, looking at an island I can't reach."

"The *Walrus*?"

"One of the ships from the book." She looked at him disapprovingly. "I thought you said you'd read *Treasure Island*? Or maybe you just looked it up on that clothesline library thingy you mentioned?"

"Well, I saw the movie. Sort of. Actually, the one I watched was set in space."

"Space?"

Jake nodded. "One of my mom's favourite movies. But the ship was called something else."

"Well, whether we're space pirates or sea pirates, we're stuck until we can figure out a way to get up there."

Jake wanted to tell Williams. But the balcony was closed. Anyone who didn't already know it was there wouldn't suspect a room was hidden in the ceiling.

Jake looked at Beth. Her eyes were locked on the *X*. She looked so eager, almost happy.

"If I had an airplane . . ."

"It's a little low for an airplane," Jake said.

"No kidding, smarty-pants," Beth said. But she was smiling.

Jake felt both a sense of pride and a jolt of fear. What if he was wrong? The *X* was unfinished. Uncarved. What if Mr. Matthewson hadn't completed whatever he was working on before he died? Had Jake just condemned Beth to another bitter disappointment?

He hoped the answer was no. He had opened up a possibility, that was all. Just a chance. But he could see that Beth believed it was true—the *X* hid one last surprise from her father.

Beth turned to look at him, her eyes wide with excitement. "We need to finish cleaning and find Mr. Williams. He'll help us look for sure."

"Definitely."

Beth hugged him. "Thanks, Jake."

Jake felt the pang of something else he couldn't quite put into words. What if he was right? If there *was* something hidden at the *X*—something he was sent to help discover—maybe he could go home. But if that happened, he would never see Beth or Williams again.

"Yeah," Jake said, forcing a smile that was bigger than he felt.

They hurried to finish cleaning up. Jake found two more unopened candy bars and stashed them in his pockets.

And when he began to dust off the upright piano, he noticed something else: a piece of paper was sticking out from underneath the bench. He reached down and pulled out a large colour poster for a movie called *Sherlock Jr.*

"Oh! That movie was hilarious. We saw it last month, before you arrived."

"Who's this Buster Keaton guy?"

Beth's jaw dropped. "Only the funniest man in the world! Well, maybe after Chaplin."

"I'll take your word for it." Jake shrugged. "Think I can keep this? I know someone who likes Sherlock Holmes a lot. A writer friend of mine."

"I don't see why not," Beth said. "But we can ask Mr. Williams about that too, just to be sure."

Jake rolled up the poster and set it aside as they put away the last of the chairs.

"All right, let's go find Mr. Williams," Beth said, slapping her hands together.

Jake stole a glance at the crossed ribs of the ceiling. His fingers tingled with excitement. They were getting close to figuring things out—he could feel it. He'd deal with the consequences—good or bad, or both—later.

They left the Great Hall and started looking for Williams. He wasn't in his basement office. Jake even activated the secret button just to be sure.

Empty.

There was no way to get into the balcony office without the key, so they went back into the Great Hall and called up to the third floor. But the panels remained closed.

They yelled louder.

"MR. WILLIAMS!!!!!!"

"Whoa, whoa! Hold your horses," said a voice from behind them.

They turned. A woman was standing in the doorway with a large wooden box on the ground next to her. She had on a grey linen dress but wore a stained smock over top.

"Yelling won't do much, except make my ears ring! I'm afraid Mr. Williams left on a business trip this morning."

Beth was crestfallen. "But . . . for how long?"

The woman shrugged. "A day? A week? The man is an enigma. I'm just here to do some painting on the ninth floor. Jeremiah said I'd need to look for someone named Jake to let me into one of the apartments up there."

"I'm Jake."

"Georgia. Nice to meet you. Do you have the key?"

He pulled it out of his pocket and handed it to the woman. "You can just leave the door unlocked and the key in the room when you're done."

"Thanks, kid. I'll be working up there for a few days. You okay with the smell of paint?"

"I guess so. You can open the windows."

The woman smiled. "Good. Well, I'm off." She lifted the wooden box and marched toward the elevator, whistling.

"I wonder what colour she's using," Jake said.

"My dad painted my room green. My favourite colour. Funny that Mr. Williams didn't ask you what colour you wanted."

They both looked back up to the empty balcony and the tantalizing X of the crossed arches.

Beth's shoulders sagged. "Well, if Mr. Williams isn't here, I guess we just have to wait."

Jake tapped her shoulder. "Of course, we could always wait while sipping a chocolate malted. My treat?"

The smile Beth gave him was worth twenty-five cents and then some.

CHAPTER NINETEEN

The smell of fresh paint was still in the air when Jake went back to his apartment, but just barely. The sounds of honking cars, neighing horses, and laughter floated through the open windows on the cool evening breeze.

As best he could in the dark, Jake avoided the drop cloth Georgia had set up along the wall. The electric lights were one thing Williams had not yet connected on the top floor. Beth had given Jake some candles, but the matches were somewhere in the kitchen. He was struggling to keep his eyes open and just wanted to collapse on his makeshift bed.

He'd check the wall colour in the morning.

He carefully rolled up the movie poster and placed it next to his other treasures under the loose floorboard in the closet. Then he pulled out his blanket and curled up into a ball on the floor of what, if the future ever came again, was going to be his room.

Jake listened to the street sounds and the chirping of birds until he fell into a deep chocolate-and-coconut-malted-induced sleep. He dreamed that he and Beth were playing baseball. She threw a fastball at his head. The ball turned into a scoop of vanilla ice cream. He hit it, and it smacked right into the ceiling of the ballroom. Drips of ice cream fell from the X in the rafters, and he and Beth ran underneath and happily caught them on their tongues like snowflakes.

Then they held hands and floated up to the X. The ceiling disappeared, and soon they were floating out over the city. The lights on the Regency's water tower twinkled like a distant star. But then their fingers slipped apart, and a gust of wind sent Beth and Jake tumbling in opposite directions. A thunderstorm flashed . . .

Jake woke up with a start. His head was spinning as he began to separate the gossamer threads of the dream from the hard floorboards below his ribs. He blinked his eyes to dissipate the feeling of fog.

The room came into focus.

A warm humid breeze flapped the loose paper on the window.

The tap was dripping slowly.

A pigeon sat on the sill, cooing.

A distant rumble of thunder sent it flying.

Jake propped himself up on his elbow and stared at the city skyline. Wait! There was no city skyline in Beth's time. Was he back home? He blinked again.

The "skyline" was actually the wall of his room. The wall that, in his time, he'd ripped the wallpaper off.

Skyscrapers rose at steep angles into a deep blue-black sky. Lights shone from below, making the buildings seem as majestic as mountains, as intimidating as giants, as light as clouds.

The tap stopped dripping and Georgia walked in from the kitchen, drying a paintbrush with a rag.

"Morning, sunshine," she said. "The door was open and I'm on a deadline, so I decided to get some more done. Did I wake you?"

Jake shook his head. "No. But . . . wait! You painted that?"

Georgia nodded.

"I thought you meant you were going to paint the walls blue or grey or something," Jake said, rubbing his eyes.

"I'm not that kind of painter." She pointed her brush at the wall. "I paint these."

"These?" Jake repeated.

"Murals. Among other things."

"It's like looking out a window," he said. "But more awesome."

"Much appreciated." Georgia gave a little bow.

"Is that the Regency?" Jake pointed to the building in the middle of the skyline. It seemed to have a halo of light around the top. Beams rose from behind like spotlights.

"Good eye. The whole scene is kind of an amalgam of different buildings from different cities that I've . . . well, kind of fallen in love with. I've painted a lot of them."

"Practice makes perfect."

"Not necessarily. To be honest, I'm thinking of a change. Of subjects and scenery. But Jeremiah heard I was in the neighbourhood and asked if I'd do a little . . . something. Before I move on."

"Little something is right. This is . . . wow!"

Georgia smiled. "Well, only a few more days of work on some of the details and you'll have a nice mural to wake up to each morning. It's painted directly on the plaster, so it should last as long as the building does." She chuckled. "Or at least as long as the wall does."

Jake felt like he'd been punched in the gut. He'd ripped that very plaster right off the wall. Why had it been covered up by wallpaper?

"You okay?"

"Sorry. Just had a weird dream, and it's sticking around in my head a bit." He got to his feet. "I'll let you keep working." He took one more look at the painting. "That really is amazing. I'll do my best to keep it safe."

"Thanks, Jake."

He had an idea. "Georgia, you don't happen to know anyone with a really tall ladder, do you?"

She raised an eyebrow. "Like I said, I'm not that kind of painter. But when Jeremiah comes back, I'm sure he can help."

"Cool. Thanks. Maybe I'll go dig around the basement."

"It's like a Minotaur's labyrinth down there. Don't break anything," Georgia said.

Jake forced a laugh. Hadn't he, in fact, been breaking and destroying things since he arrived at the Regency? Both now and in his own time?

He'd ripped the plaster off his wall.

He'd raised Beth's hopes with no way to satisfy them.

He'd forced Williams to face memories he clearly hadn't wanted to face.

He'd been mean to his mom.

Maybe everything he was trying to do to help was making things worse?

Jake walked into the hallway and slowly closed the door

behind him. He rested his forehead on the cool wood of the jamb.

Maybe he was wrong about what he was doing here? Maybe he was wrong about everything? Once he had accepted that he'd gone back in time, he'd assumed it was to do something good, something to save the building. But when he saw the beautiful painting that he'd one day destroy, a new thought occurred to him.

Maybe he had been sent back here as punishment?

Maybe the building was teaching him a lesson?

And maybe there was nothing he could do to get back home. Maybe he *was* trapped. He'd wondered that first day in the balcony if he'd died and gone to heaven. Maybe it was the opposite?

Jake lifted his head and yelled down the empty hallway. "Is that what you want? Am I in prison or something? Well . . . I'M SORRY, OKAY?!"

His voice was swallowed up by the halls and the carpet. The door to his apartment slid open a crack, and Georgia peeked out at him.

"Jake, you okay?"

"Sorry. I was just checking out the acoustics." He remembered Louis Armstrong using that word when they chatted, although he wasn't one hundred percent sure what it meant.

"Well, my ears can attest that they are pretty good." She closed the door.

"C'mon, Regency, just tell me what you want," Jake said in a whisper.

The hallway and the carpet didn't answer.

"Fine." He took a deep breath and marched to the elevator, where he pressed *B*.

The elevator descended to the basement, and Jake stepped out. There was a sharp clang and a crash to his right. Someone else was down here. A robber?

Jake decided that it was better to be safe than sorry. He spotted a huge metal wrench propped against the closest boiler tank. He slid down the wall, crept across the floor, and picked it up. Then he slid between the pipes and oil tanks until he got to where the noises were coming from. Someone was sliding boxes around, grunting with the effort.

Jake clutched the wrench like a bat and lifted his head over the top of a low wall of boxes.

Something metal clanged off the concrete floor and then spun to a stop.

"ARGH!" said a familiar voice.

Jake's head popped up. "Beth?"

Beth was standing in the middle of a pile of pipes and tubes, looking dirty and mad, holding what appeared to be a brass doorknob.

She was so surprised by Jake's sudden appearance that she threw the doorknob straight at him. He swung the wrench and fouled off the orb. It sailed away, straight through one of the small basement windows.

Glass fragments rained down on the floor.

"Oops," Jake said with a frown.

Beth actually laughed. "So you *can* play!"

"Was that a fastball?"

Beth nodded. "Not my best, clearly."

"Ouch."

"So what are you doing down here?" they asked at the same time.

Jake pointed at Beth. "You go first."

"In all things." She smiled. "I'm down here looking for some way—"

"To get up there and see what's in the ceiling." Jake finished the sentence. "Me too. You know, Beth, there might be nothing up there. I could be wrong."

Beth glared at him. "Jake, let me dream a little, okay?"

"Sorry," he said. "So what are we looking for?"

"Scaffolding. A ladder. A rope. Something. There's got to be a way to get up there. I mean, how do the cleaners dust?"

"Have you ever seen anyone dusting?"

"THAT'S NOT THE POINT!" Beth kicked a piece of pipe. It skidded away across the floor. "Are you going to help or not?"

Jake put down the wrench, and they began searching through the basement for anything that might help them get close to the ceiling.

And finally, they found something. Tucked at the far end of the basement, close to the service elevator, there was a row of metal pipes. Some were still attached in sections and panels.

"That's scaffolding?"

"Well, you have to put it together," Beth said.

"And you know how?"

She picked up some of the pipes and turned them over in her hands. "How hard can it be?"

CHAPTER TWENTY

Hard, as it turned out. And impossible for two kids. Beth and Jake spent most of the day loading the elevator with pieces and then lugging them into the Great Hall.

But all they ended up with was a pile of pipes in the middle of the ballroom floor.

"Looks like all the plumbing in the building had a wild party," Beth said.

"There are no movies or concerts tonight, right?" Jake asked, staring helplessly at the pile. "'Cause I don't think we're getting anywhere near there." He pointed at the X. It seemed even farther away than it had the morning before.

"My dad used to say you never know how bad an idea is until you try it out," Beth said.

"That does not fill me with confidence."

"You are such a wet noodle sometimes."

Jake rubbed the sweat off his forehead. "I'm just a little worried. Beth, seriously. I keep screwing things up. What if this is all just a huge mistake?"

She looked at him for a long time before speaking. "Jake, we all mess up. Okay? All the time."

"You definitely messed up on that curveball to Cool Papa Bell."

She frowned. "Very funny. What I'm saying is that if you *were* sent here, it was to do something good. You've warned Mr. Williams about the Regency. And you've warned *me*. And trust me, I'm going to keep an eye on this place. You promised you would too, remember?"

Jake remembered. "What if I can't?"

"Well, what IF you can't?" She stared at him, waiting for an answer, but Jake wasn't sure what to say.

"Then what am I doing here?"

"Trying. Doing the best you can."

"Okay." Jake's lip trembled. "Thanks."

"Now let's see if we can turn this pile into something useful." Beth clapped her hands. "The parts must fit together like Lincoln Logs or an Erector Set."

"Whatever those are." Jake looked at the parts that were still connected. "These pipes are locked into each other with some kind of T-shaped joining thingy."

"Joining thingy? Very technical."

"Well, what would you call it?"

"A . . . connector thingy."

She picked up a long pipe and slipped it into the slot on the left side of the *T*. "Now I put one in the right side and one in the bottom, and it should work. At least I think so."

"You *think*?"

"I visited my dad every day when he was in here, and that's basically what it looked like." She tried to stand up a section of the piping, but it rattled and collapsed. "Hmm, that didn't work."

"Maybe if I hold one side?"

"Good idea." Beth reassembled the pieces and then Jake held that section while Beth slid more pipes and joints together. They talked as they built.

"I'd bring my dad his lunch, and he'd use a rope to pull it up to the top."

"How did he get up there?" Jake asked, doing his best to hold his side together.

"He climbed up the outside. I think there's a ladder or something built into the side of some of the sections."

"You said 'I think' again."

"Jake, thinking is how you figure things out."

"Uh-huh."

Once they had built two long sections, they attached two smaller sections at each end, forming a kind of rectangle of joined pipe about six feet high.

Beth slid a final length of pipe into the T-shaped connector above Jake's head, then stepped back. "Okay, let go."

Jake let go. The sections wobbled but stayed together.

"Yes!" they said.

Jake held up his hand to give Beth a high five. She stared at his hand, confused.

"Did you see a mosquito or something?"

"Never mind," Jake said. He lowered his hand and patted Beth on the shoulder. "Just trying to say how happy I am."

"By slapping me on the head?" She rolled her eyes and looked back at the finished section. "That's one floor done." Beth planted her hands on her hips.

"Um, how many more to go?"

Beth looked up. "Five? Ten?"

Jake gulped.

Then the wobble became more of a sway and the section of scaffolding fell down sideways. The longest pipe bounced free and rolled away across the floor, banging against the far wall.

"Ugh." Jake slumped to the floor. "I need ice cream."

Beth kicked a smaller pipe, which skipped across the floor and clanged against the doors. The doors opened.

"What in blazes was that?!" said a deep voice.

"Mr. Williams! You're back!"

He made a show of looking at his hands and arms. "It would appear so."

Beth and Jake ran over and hugged him.

"Thanks, you two." Then he noticed the pile of pipes in the middle of his ballroom. "Wait a minute! I'm not sure I want to pay you to clean up messes that you make."

"We had a good reason," Beth said.

"Which is?"

Jake and Beth practically burst out with their news. They told Williams about the angels, the X at the heart of the building, and the possibility that Beth's father had hidden something there.

"And we were just getting ready to find the buried treasure!" Beth was almost hopping from foot to foot.

But Williams frowned as he stared up at the X in the ceiling. "Hmm. I'm not so sure. I watched Charles working on this ceiling for months. The wood is bare. Maybe he intended to do such a thing but ran out of time?" He placed a hand on Beth's shoulder and gave a gentle squeeze.

"No," she said. "No. Something is up there."

Williams looked at Jake. "You're sure about all this?"

Jake had hoped he wouldn't be asked that question, because he wasn't sure. He hadn't been completely sure of anything since he'd opened the door to apartment 713. But then he caught a glimpse of Beth's face. She was pleading with him the same way he'd pleaded with her that first day. They needed Williams to help them.

"Yes," Jake said, trying to sound more confident than he felt. "One hundred percent. Something is there."

Beth smiled at him.

Williams sighed. "Okay. Here's what I'll do. You two get this old scaffolding lugged back downstairs. No, put it out back. I should have had it sent to the dump ages ago."

"Dump?"

"There have been some improvements to the clamps and fittings since . . . well, since Charles used it."

"See?" said Beth. "It wasn't our fault the stuff didn't fit together."

"I wouldn't go that far," Williams said. "But it's finicky. To be honest, your dad was probably the only one who could fit it together and make it work. I kept telling him we should replace it, but he said there wasn't . . . time." Williams looked back up at the crossed arches and took a deep breath.

Then he smiled at Jake and Beth. "I'll call some friends of mine to come and take a look. Deal?"

Beth nodded vigorously.

"They'll look. Not *you*."

Jake and Beth looked at each other sadly.

"The thrill of discovery isn't as much fun when someone else is doing the discovering," Beth said.

"I'm not having two kids climbing up to the ceiling. We'll let the professionals handle this. It'll take a few days, but then we'll see what there is to see. If there is anything to see."

"Okay."

"And to be honest, it's about time that section gets painted to match the rest of the room. I didn't really have the heart to do it before. But I think your dad would have liked to see it finished."

"But they'll look first, right?"

Williams nodded. "I will make sure the painters have a good look. If there is something hidden up there, they'll find it."

"It will be there," Beth said. "I know it."

"Now if you'll excuse me, I'm late for some meetings."

He walked away, looking back at the ceiling as he closed the doors of the hall.

"So," Beth said after a long silence, "you mentioned something about treating me to ice cream?"

"Treating?"

CHAPTER TWENTY-ONE

It turned out that the painters couldn't come right away, so the Great Hall was still, in Beth's words, "open for business." And the crossing arches remained tantalizingly far away even as the hall itself shook with energy.

Williams packed in new entertainments for every available night.

"Who doesn't love a good party?" he told the kids. "And they also help provide an education to the people who live here. They should all have a sense of the possibilities of the wide, wide world."

"And it gives us a few more paydays cleaning up after all the ticket-buying slobs," Beth said.

"And a chance at more unopened candy bars," Jake added with a smile. He suspected that Williams was also trying to distract himself from thoughts of what the painters might, or might not, find.

There were more movies, including a German vampire movie called *Nosferatu* that Jake had to admit was as scary as any vampire movie he'd seen, even without sound and colour.

There were more concerts from famous musicians. Williams introduced them to Beth and Jake, but always by their first names: George, Ira, Bix, Bessie, Duke. The one named Duke turned out to be the man in the wide-brimmed hat who had smiled at Jake that first afternoon in the hallway outside Beth's apartment. Jake still didn't know who he was, but he did play a mean piano. Jake figured he could ask Theo or do a Google search when he got back home.

He didn't need to google Albert Einstein, though—he recognized his crazy hair and bushy moustache. His science teacher, Ms. Berot, had a poster of the genius on the wall of her lab.

Einstein came to the Great Hall and gave a lecture on space that inspired Beth and Jake to spend a night on the roof with a telescope. They saw glorious meteor showers and aligning planets.

How did Williams know Einstein? It turned out the physicist had helped design, of all things, the refrigeration system in the Regency's kitchens. "No one else took my idea seriously," he told Jake and Beth after his speech. "They all thought I should stick to physics! But Jeremiah thinks differently from so many other people."

Jake asked the scientist if he believed in the possibility of other Earths, and Einstein jotted down some thoughts on the back of a piece of scrap paper. Jake had no idea what the letters and scribbles meant, but he was pretty sure that Professor Friendly would.

Beth was diving into the educational opportunities with both feet.

She'd asked Georgia to help her learn how to draw better.

Then other artists had shown up to decorate the rest of the ninth-floor apartments, and Beth had hounded each of them—resulting in a sketchbook filled with new designs for paintings, carvings, and sculptures.

At first, Jake tagged along because Beth wanted him to. But he found himself enjoying all the cool bits of knowledge he was picking up about art, music, science.

The weirdest event, though—at least to Jake—was the dance marathon. Couples would dance until they collapsed or got tagged out by a judge for not moving their feet enough. The winning couple lasted almost twenty-four hours and won a whopping hundred dollars.

Jake and Beth had entered—it cost a quarter—but they got tagged out after only fifteen minutes when Jake tripped over Beth's feet. They sat and ate popcorn and watched the other dancers until it was almost midnight.

Beth called it a "bunion derby."

"Because all the *good* dancers end up with sores on their feet from dancing for so long." She told Jake there were some marathons that went on for weeks.

Jake rubbed his toes. "I can't think of a worse form of torture."

And every night, Jake fell asleep gazing at Georgia's mural of a glowing, brilliant imaginary skyline. The Regency and its halo of light lingered into his dreams.

How could he make sure this would still be here when he finally got back? If he ever got back. He was starting to feel like that might never happen. It had been weeks. If he was gone much longer, the deadline for saving the place would pass. If he was stuck here for months, the demolition would have already begun.

He was surprised to find that his anxiety actually made the time pass *more* slowly, as slow as molasses.

Jake knew exactly how slow that was because Beth had convinced him to help her make molasses cookies for all the residents of the Regency.

"I think this stuff is in slo-mo," Jake had said, watching the thick brown liquid take forever to escape from its tin can.

"Slow-what?"

"Never mind. Why not just get premade dough?"

"You know, the future sounds speedier but not as much fun," Beth said. "Remember what Chef Boiardi said? Patience. Patience."

Chef Boiardi, the head chef at some famous hotel restaurant, was another guest Williams had brought in. The chef had made an amazing buffet for the neighbourhood and given Jake a signed recipe for almond biscotti—made out to Delaney.

"Finally!" Beth said as Jake used a wooden spoon to get the last of the molasses out of the tin and into the bowl.

"Now what?" he said.

"You mix." She handed Jake a whisk.

"Me?"

"You need the exercise. You still can't throw the ball from the outfield to home plate."

"Don't need to make that throw if I catch the ball before it hits the ground." He handed Beth the whisk. "Your fastball has been a little slooooow. Maybe *you* need the exercise."

"Fine, we'll take turns."

No more famous baseball players had popped in to say hi, but the sandlot games had continued almost every afternoon. Jake was actually getting pretty good at guessing, just from the sound of the bat, where the ball was heading. He looked forward to the games.

He also liked the daily walks in this strange new—or, he figured, *old*—world, and the inevitable ice cream at the end.

"It used to be tough to get you outside," Beth had joked. "Now I can't get you back in."

She seemed to have gone the other way, spending more and more time in the hall, staring up every day at the *X* in the ballroom ceiling. She didn't want to be away from the Regency for long, almost as if she worried it might not be there when she got back.

The front door clicked open.

Beth's mom walked in.

Jake dropped the whisk onto the floor. She wasn't due home for hours, and he had planned to be long gone by then.

"Jake!" She placed a brown box on the counter. "How is your mother?"

Jake tried to avoid her gaze by leaning down to pick up the whisk in his shaking hands. "Um. Great? She's been working a lot lately."

"Working where? And what does she do again?"

"Uh, she's a legal secretary."

"So do the lawyers work as late as the secretaries at her office?"

"Um . . . uh . . . yes?"

Beth tried to steer the conversation toward safer waters. "Why are you home so early?"

"I'm just dropping in on my way back to the Mulvaneys' house. I got some treats from the butcher, and they need to go in the icebox right away."

"We can do that, Mother," Beth said. "What are they?"

"It was such good timing. I went to the butcher's to buy some steaks. The Mulvaneys are having a big party this weekend. Mr. Gasparo said he had some extra cuts left over." She held up a brown paper package with "Veal" written on it in dark pencil.

"Jellied veal!" Beth said. She leapt into her mother's arms.

Jake was confused. What was so exciting about jelly?

Beth released her mom. They were both sniffling, their eyes damp.

"It was Dad's favourite," Beth said. "It's been so long."

"Too long," her mom said, brushing a hand through Beth's curls. "I hope I remember the proper way to cook it! Now I need you to run down to the lobby and grab some fresh ice before the meat goes bad."

Beth nodded. "On it. You coming, Jake?"

"Jake can stay here with me," Mrs. Matthewson said. "Now run along."

Beth hesitated but squeaked out the words "Yes, Mother," then turned and walked quickly down the hall.

Jake was now alone in the kitchen with Mrs. Matthewson. She turned slowly to face him.

"Jake?" she said, smiling a huge smile.

He gulped. "Yes, ma'am?"

She leaned toward him, and he backed away. "Thank you."

He wasn't expecting that. "Thank me?"

She laid a gentle hand on his and patted it. "Ever since Charles's death"—she paused to compose herself—"ever since that time, Beth has been low. She doesn't always seem that way, but a mother sees. Lord knows that I have tried to help her. But with work and more work and trying to find a better life . . ." She wiped away a tear.

Jake thought again of his own mother. "It's been hard for you too."

She nodded, wiping her eyes on her shirtsleeve. "Yes, it has. But what I see in her eyes now. Her energy. Her sparkle. She used to draw all the time with her father. She hadn't even tried since he died. Now she's back. And especially the last few days, she's seemed so hopeful. Maybe even happy. And that is a girl I have missed."

Jake's throat went dry. *The last few days.* He knew what had changed Beth, and it wasn't him. It was the hope of a message from her father.

He had to believe they would find something in the ceiling. The alternative made him shudder. How deep a fall might it be—for Beth and for him—if that hope turned out to be misplaced.

Beth's mother had continued talking to him, but Jake had missed some of it until he heard ". . . may be time for a move."

"Wait, what?"

"Mr. Williams has shown us such kindness since Charles's death. To be honest, I knew he would watch over her, but living alone so much can get a child into trouble. If anything ever happened to her . . ." She wiped away another tear. "But our little flower has grown up. And maybe it's time to go search for that better place."

Jake fought a rising sense of panic. "Move? But Beth loves the Regency. This is her home."

Mrs. Matthewson waved her hand in the air. "It's just a thought. Charles and I never intended to stay here forever. It was a place to start, a place on the way to other things. That's what he and Jeremiah had always wanted to build." She nodded her head firmly and patted Jake's hand again. "Anyway, I have to get back to work. When Beth returns, can you make sure the veal is put in the icebox?"

"You're making jelly with the *meat*?" Now Jake was even less sure why anyone would be excited.

"You'll love it. I expect you and your mother to join us for dinner tomorrow night. And this time I will not take no for an answer."

Jake struggled to come up with a new excuse. "She's working late."

"Then we will wait until she is done. But I need to ask her some questions. Is she avoiding us for any reason?" Beth's mom looked almost hurt at the idea.

"No, no. It's not that. She's just really busy. Really, really busy. And she has to travel for work a lot. She's actually away now."

"Without her son? Hmmm."

Jake wanted to smack himself. Beth had warned him what happened to street urchins who got reported to the authorities. He needed to be careful. "She's back tomorrow," he said quickly.

"Jake, a mother needs to meet the mother of her child's new best friend."

"Okay."

"Or else, maybe she won't trust that friend anymore." She fixed her eyes on his and folded her arms. It was the same look Beth had given him that first afternoon in the apartment, but with more menace.

"Okay." Jake nodded.

"Good." She tied up her coat and began walking away. "Dinner. Tomorrow."

Jake stared after her, dumbfounded. She closed the door, leaving him alone in the kitchen. And where was Beth? How long did it take to grab a block of ice?

He waited for a few more minutes and was just about to go looking for her when she burst through the door.

"Jake! The workers are here, and they've started putting up the scaffolding!"

"That's amazing!"

"Mr. Williams says it will take a couple of days." She put down the ice and hugged him. "We're so close."

Her fingers were freezing, but to Jake, it was the warmest of hugs.

CHAPTER TWENTY-TWO

The dinner wobbled. Jake poked it with his fork. It wobbled more. Chunks of veal hung suspended in a kind of green-grey jelly.

Beth's mom was in the kitchen, finishing up the boiled potatoes and what Beth called her signature macaroni and cheese.

Jake had shown up early and said his mom would join them later. But now he wasn't sure he wanted to stay. Not just because of how badly things might go, but also because of the unsettling appearance of his wobbling food.

He leaned in close to Beth and whispered, "So what is this, exactly?"

"Aspic," Beth said, licking her lips for effect.

"Ass-what?"

"Aspic. It's a kind of jelly. All the radio shows say it's très élégante."

"It's Jell-O with meat in it."

"So?"

"Do you have ketchup? Or maybe whipped cream? Or a hungry dog or cat? It actually looks like cat food."

"You've eaten cat food?"

"No. I just take care of some cats. They're really sweet, actually. And they'd love me to give them some of that." He jabbed the aspic with his fork, setting it jiggling again.

Beth narrowed her eyes. "It's a delicacy."

"Not where I come from."

"It was also my dad's favourite dish, and we haven't had it in years. This is a big step for my mom. So . . . any more questions?"

"I. Can't. Wait," Jake said, forcing a smile. He figured he could always fill up on the fresh biscuits and butter and leave the aspic for Beth and her mom . . . and his mom.

Mrs. Matthewson came in from the kitchen with a pan of what appeared to be baked spaghetti and cheese. Jake's stomach grumbled. He was hungry. Not enough to wolf down the jelly thing, but this actually looked and smelled amazing. He missed real food.

He'd been able to feed himself, a bit. He'd bought some bread and cheese from Mr. Chan across the street, but it didn't last long. Jake was no cook. And despite repeated searches, he'd had no luck finding a pizza shop.

"So, Jake, when should we expect your mother to arrive?" Mrs. Matthewson went back to the kitchen to grab the potatoes.

Jake and Beth exchanged a quick glance.

"Any time now," Jake said. "She just got back from her trip this afternoon, and she's very excited to finally meet you. The last time I saw her, she was getting dressed up."

Mrs. Matthewson placed the bowl of steaming spuds on the table and took her seat. Jake was about to stab one when she tsked. "It would be rude to eat without all our guests here. Be patient. Unless your mother is not coming?"

Jake gulped, pulled back his fork, and stared at the door, a bead of sweat rolling down his neck. "She said she'd be here by seven."

They were quiet for a bit. The clock on the wall ticked loudly. It was two minutes past seven.

Beth's mom spoke up. "So anything new in the building? More concerts?"

Jake was happy for the change in topic. "Well, the hall is closed while the workers set up the scaffolding."

Beth's mom gave a startled shake. "Scaffolding? Why?"

Beth kicked him under the table. She'd avoided telling her mom anything about the X or the mystery they were trying to solve. There hadn't been scaffolding in that room since her father's death.

"Um, it's for a play or something, I think."

"A play? Why not do it on the stage?" She raised an eyebrow, clearly suspicious. Her natural state, Beth once told Jake.

"It's a new experimental theatre group," Beth said. "They're here from Europe."

"Where in Europe, exactly?"

Jake had to give it to Beth's mom. She was persistent.

"Russia," Jake said.

"Russia? You mean the Soviet Union?"

Jake wasn't sure what that was, but he nodded. "It's like a circus. They're acrobats, so the scaffolding is for their acts and stuff."

"I'll have to ask Jeremiah about this," said Beth's mom, and Jake urgently hoped she wouldn't. "I might be wrong, but I didn't know anyone from there was allowed to travel."

Jake and Beth exchanged a worried glance. This was starting to veer into dangerous territory.

"JAKE!" came a sugary voice from the doorway.

"Just in the nick of time," Beth whispered.

"Is this the right apartment?" The person in the doorway seemed to be mostly coat and hat, the face obscured by a furry scarf. Strands of black hair peeked out from the hat.

"Mom?" Jake said. "I mean, MOM! Come in." His eyes quickly darted from his "mom" to Beth and back again. Jake had never seen the person before, but Beth had assured him this wacky plan could work.

"Mrs. Simmons, I presume?" said Beth's mom, sliding back her chair and extending her hand.

"Bernice. And you must be Beth's mother. Jake has told me so much about you." Bernice slipped off the scarf and hat, and Beth's mom hung them up in the hall closet.

"So tell me a little bit about Jake," Beth's mom said, offering her guest a seat.

Jake and Beth took this as their cue to finally fill their plates.

"What is there to say, really? He's a little scamp. But a sweetie." Bernice reached across the table and pinched Jake's cheeks, winking at him.

"And Jake's father?"

Bernice paused for a second and stole a glance at Jake, who was frozen with panic. He'd given Beth a page of cheat notes, but having never had a father, he hadn't thought to prep this one.

Bernice improvised. "Out of the picture. But I don't need to tell you about the difficulties of raising a child alone."

They smiled at each other and then began filling their own plates.

"Oh, I dropped my fork," Jake said, dropping his fork to the ground.

"Oh no," Beth said.

The kids reached for it at the same time, and Jake grimaced at Beth under the table.

"Are you sure your mom isn't a cop or something?"

"I told you, she just wants to make sure you're not trouble— or *in* trouble."

"I'm doomed."

Mrs. Matthewson's face appeared under the tablecloth. "Is everything okay down there?"

"Found it!" Beth said, grabbing the fork.

All three heads popped back up.

Bernice gave a throaty laugh. "Just like meerkats in a *National Geographic* photo!"

"Do you read a lot of magazines?" Beth's mom asked.

"Darling, I adore them! And anything that helps little Jack's imagination grow."

"You mean Jake?"

Bernice didn't flinch. "Little Jack is one of my pet names for my sweet boy."

Bernice was impressive, dodging question after question from Mrs. Matthewson. Maybe Jake wasn't doomed?

Beth's mom continued the interrogation between bites.

"You have such lovely nails for someone who spends all day typing."

Again, Bernice didn't miss a beat. "I'm more of a stenographer. Pencil and paper. And I have a secret I need to confess."

Jake gulped. Had Beth's mom cracked their not-so-carefully-constructed plan?

But Bernice reached out and took hold of Mrs. Matthewson's hand, examining the lines and cracks. "Honey, your work is wearing out these lovely digits."

Beth's mom looked hurt and pulled her hand back. "There's nothing wrong with hard work."

Bernice grabbed the hand again and stroked it gently. "Sorry, dear. That's not at all what I meant. I too have suffered cracks and dryness, but I have discovered a magic elixir."

"Elixir?"

Bernice nodded. "Edna Wallace Hopper."

"The actress?" Beth's mom looked confused.

Jake, of course, had never heard of her, but Beth and her mom clearly had.

Bernice nodded. "She has developed a hand cream that works wonders, absolute WONDERS. I have some in my bag." Bernice reached down and pulled out a small red tin with a picture of a woman's face on the label. "A gift to you. For being so kind to my little boy."

Beth's mom clutched the tin like she'd been given a golden ring. "I am speechless. This is so kind of you. Thank you so much!"

The rest of dinner passed without any more interrogating, and Bernice filled the time telling stories about how Jake had been such a difficult baby, how he almost broke his arm chasing after a dogcatcher, how he never played hooky (whatever that was).

"You'd better be keeping notes," Beth whispered to Jake, passing him the butter.

"No kidding."

He was worried that Bernice was laying it on too thick, but Beth's mom laughed and eventually joined in with her own stories about Beth. How Beth's teachers described her as "headstrong" and "intelligent," and how both might get her into trouble some-day. Beth just smirked.

Jake relaxed as dinner went on. Only once did he regret the plan—when Bernice gushed about how much Jake *loved* aspic, and Beth had taken that as her cue to slop a thick slice onto his plate.

The first mouthful had gone down okay, aided by a heaping pile of salt, but the second reminded him of Anastasia's cat food and he had to suppress a gag. He jammed the rest into his mouth in one lump, then excused himself and ran to the bathroom.

A spit and a flush later, Jake felt better. He rummaged through the cabinet and found a tube of toothpaste and rinsed his mouth. At least, he hoped it was toothpaste. It tasted more like chalk.

Jake got back just as Mrs. Matthewson was saying, "Beth used to draw a lot with her father, but she stopped. That is, until Jake showed up."

Even from behind, Jake could see Beth blush.

"Okay, Mom," Jake said. "We should go."

Bernice seemed genuinely disappointed. But Jake gave a loud yawn, which was the secret signal to end the night before any slip-ups. He already had about twenty new childhood memories he was going to have to learn.

"Yes." Bernice yawned as well. "An early start tomorrow. Thank you so much for a wonderful dinner."

They walked to the door together.

Mrs. Matthewson smiled. "Well, Jake, thank you for finally letting me meet your wonderful mother."

"Uh-huh," Jake said, moving his "mom" closer to the door.

"It was an enchanting evening," Bernice said. "And we must do this again soon. Perhaps at our place next time?"

Jake couldn't stop a panicked squeak from escaping his lips.

"Mice?" Beth said, trying her best to cover it up.

"Not in my apartment!" said her mom.

"Maybe you should get a cat," Bernice suggested.

"Beth has always wanted one. But I'm afraid that is a luxury I can't afford. Dinner would be lovely. Should we pick a date now?"

Bernice coughed. "Of course. I am on the road a fair amount. But by all means when I return. I will be in touch. I'm sure Jake would love to show you *his* favourite aspic recipe. It's tuna."

"That sounds perfect," said Beth's mom.

"Bye!" Jake said.

He closed the door and walked Bernice to the elevator. They didn't speak until the doors had closed and they were alone.

"This boring mom hair wig is not very comfortable," Bernice said, sliding it off to reveal a short-cropped haircut. "Here. You can have it. It's far *too* boring for my act."

"Thanks. Um, how much do I owe you?"

"I believe your friend said ten dollars."

"Right." Jake pulled out a sock filled with coins. Most of his savings was now gone.

"Charming," Bernice said, putting on a long glove and pinching the sock. "But of course, that was before I gave up my precious hand cream. Another dollar and we can call it even."

Jake fumbled around in his pocket for the extra coins and handed them to Bernice.

"Thank you, Jake. That Beth friend of yours must really care about you to set this all up." Bernice stared in the mirror, licked a finger, and tucked an eyelash back in line.

"Beth is amazing."

"Brave too. It's not any kid who'll walk into my club yelling, 'I need a mom.'" Bernice burst out laughing so hard the eyelash drooped again.

"Is Bernice your real name?"

"Stage name. My real name is Francis Renault."

"Glad to meet you, Francis. And thanks for being my mom. It means a lot."

"Just make sure her mother doesn't catch my revue at the Pigeon Club next week or we're both cooked."

"I don't think that will be a problem," Jake said. He wasn't sure what kind of place the Pigeon Club was, but he was pretty sure it wasn't the type Beth's mom would visit.

The elevator door opened, and Francis gave Jake a wave and then walked away. Jake pressed the button for the ninth floor, and the door slid closed.

He had dodged a huge challenge for the time being, but now what?

"Okay, Regency," he said to the empty elevator, "are you happy yet?"

The only response was the sound of cables carrying him back to his apartment.

CHAPTER TWENTY-THREE

Jake woke up with a splitting headache. And he was cold. He shivered, trying in vain to wrap himself more tightly in his thin blanket. A breeze rustled the curtains over his head, sending drops of water onto his cheek.

Jake wiped the drops away. He and his blanket were soaked. "What the—?"

There was a flash of lightning and a tremendous boom of thunder. More rain blew inside. Jake forced himself to his feet and shut the window. More lightning and more thunder. Standing and moving seemed to take the edge off the throbbing in his temple, although a bright flash and rumble did make him squint with momentary pain.

A thunderstorm had clearly settled over the Regency. Jake squeezed his eyes shut and tried to remember why that was significant.

More lightning and thunder. And then. . . muffled cheers?

Jake peeked out the window. A group of kids were huddled in the entranceway of the grocery store across the street. They were pointing up at his window.

He quickly checked to make sure he hadn't forgotten to get dressed.

Another flash of lightning sent the kids in the doorway jumping up and down. The owner of the store, Mr. Chan, came out. Jake expected him to chase the loitering kids away, but he joined them in staring up at the building.

The skies opened up. The kids and Mr. Chan got soaked, and finally Jake remembered. Electric candy floss, Beth had called it. The kids weren't pointing at him—they were pointing at the roof of the Regency.

Beth had told him to come find her the next time he heard thunder. Or was she going to find him? It was supposed to be like watching nature's fireworks.

So why hadn't she come and grabbed him?

He looked outside again to see if she was one of the kids across the street. But they had run away, or gone inside, as soon as the rain began coming down.

There was another flash of lightning, but this time the thunder followed a second or so later. The storm was quickly moving away. He'd missed it. His head started throbbing again. What time was it? It felt like the middle of the night, but the grocery store was open. As the clouds began to rumble away, more sunlight peeked through and lit up puddles and wet streets. Bikes, cars, and horses began to appear, delivering milk bottles, bread, papers.

Morning for sure. Midmorning? Morning.

He stumbled to the bathroom. Workers had now installed a tub, so Jake sat in the warm water and let his body wake up. His headache dissolved bit by bit.

He kept expecting Beth to interrupt him with a loud knock

on the door, but the water had cooled considerably by the time he was ready to get on with the day.

Wrapped in a towel, also borrowed from Beth's apartment, Jake walked across the floor, leaving wet footprints on the smooth planks. The storm clouds had gone, and sunlight now streamed into the room.

Jake, who had felt close to death just a short time before, was refreshed and alive. *The scaffolding must be up by now*, he thought. He and Beth had satisfied her mom's suspicions, at least for the time being. Whatever the Regency wanted from him, he had to be close to providing. He'd be home soon. He could feel it.

But his happiness at the thought was still tinged with sadness. He sat on the floor and pulled on his socks and wondered what should happen next.

Maybe Beth could come back to the future with him? Her mom would come too, of course. He smiled as he imagined Beth doing her first Google search or playing her first video game. Or going to art school, where being "intelligent" and "headstrong" would be good things. Maybe, if he asked her, she'd say yes? She loved adventure.

He was just pulling on his shirt when he heard a loud bang on the door. Was Beth using a hammer?

"Hold your horses!" Jake called.

A deep voice boomed through the thick wood. "Jake, it's Mr. Williams. I need your help right away."

There was no missing the panic in Williams's voice. Jake quickly poked his head through his hoodie and rushed to the door. He flung it open so hard that the architect almost fell inside.

"Have you seen Beth?"

Jake felt his headache coming back. "No. Why?"

"I've made a mess of everything," Williams said.

"What? How?"

Williams leaned against the doorframe, rubbing his forehead. "The painters."

Jake felt a trembling, as if the floor were starting to heave. "What about the painters?"

"They took a look." He took a deep breath. "There was nothing there."

"No, no. That's not possible."

The room seemed to spin. All Jake's hopes were pinned on this. His knees wobbled, and he grabbed Williams by the sleeve to steady himself.

"Sorry, Jake." Williams put a hand on his shoulder and squeezed. "I know it's hard to accept, but they got to the top and looked all around. There was nothing there."

"Nothing?"

"Just the two arches, untouched except for some pencil marks Charles made before he died. Plans for carvings that he never even began."

"The pencil marks must have been something, no? Writing? A message?" Jake could hear the desperation in his own voice.

Williams shook his head. "They were just rough outlines. The same method he used in the rest of the hall. Except Charles ran out of time and . . ." Williams paused to catch his breath. "I know I didn't seem to share your enthusiasm, but I did. I had such hope that you and Beth were right. But I was worried that it would feel like I'd lost Charles again if we found nothing. And it does."

There was a rumble of thunder. Another storm was approaching the Regency. The dark clouds rolled in quickly, blocking the light from the windows.

Williams rubbed his temples and seemed ready to sink into the wall.

Jake marvelled at how such a large man could appear so small when grief hit him in the gut. Jake also felt like he'd been punched.

"Wait—you came here looking for Beth. Why?"

Williams stood up slowly. "I went to her apartment and told her what the painters had told me."

"Oh no." Jake felt like the air had been sucked out of his lungs.

Williams nodded. "She began crying and ran past me. I couldn't catch her. I had hoped that she'd run here."

Jake shook his head. "Did you call Figueredo's?"

"Yes. She hasn't been there."

The thunderstorm had washed out any chance of a baseball game. If Beth was hiding somewhere out there, the chances of finding her were slim.

A flash of lightning and a boom of thunder shook the building.

Jake had a horrible thought. "Where are the painters now?"

"Out. They'll start work this afternoon."

"Did they leave the scaffolding up?"

"Yes."

Jake raised an eyebrow, and Williams shuddered. "No. She wouldn't."

"She one hundred percent would."

"But the door is locked."

"This is Beth we're talking about," Jake said.

Without another word, Jake and Williams turned and ran down the hall.

"We'll take the service elevator," Williams called. "It opens directly into the hall." He tossed the key.

Jake snatched it out of the air like a line drive and, in one motion, slid it into the lock. The doors opened instantly.

Jake pushed the button for the second floor just as Williams slipped inside.

They descended, but each floor seemed to take a decade to pass.

Finally the doors slid apart. The hall was dark, the clouds outside choking the sunlight.

"BETH!" Jake called. There was no answer. His voice seemed to be swallowed by the gloom. "BETH?!"

"I'll get the lights," Williams said. He walked away into the darkness.

Just then, a flash of lightning illuminated the scaffolding, which rose like a skeleton to the ceiling.

"BETH!" Jake called again.

Thunder and another flash of lightning filled the room with blue light, and Jake's eyes were drawn to the floor by the base of the steel pipes.

Something was there. A dark mound. No, a person, with arms and legs twisted at odd angles.

Jake ran over, his heart pounding.

Beth lay motionless on the floor.

CHAPTER TWENTY-FOUR

Williams pushed the switch and the lights came up just as Jake reached Beth. Her face was obscured by her arm, and her hair was matted with blood. Her limbs seemed even more twisted now that Jake was up close.

"Beth?" He was afraid to touch her. She seemed like a broken glass, and he had no idea how to put her back together. "Beth, you bonehead," he sobbed, reaching out to straighten her arms and then pulling his hand back. "Why didn't you come get me?"

He looked up at the vaulted ceiling. The X was barely visible, unreachable. Had she fallen from the top? Had she even made it halfway before slipping? Had she slipped on the way down?

Did it matter? Did anything matter now?

He was filled with an urge to pound his fists through the floor, to take a sledgehammer to the carvings, the vaults, the whole damn building.

He stood up and screamed at the walls. "Are you happy?"

Thunder rumbled overhead.

"Is this what you wanted? You stupid . . . DUMP!"

More lightning and thunder, and the lights flickered.

Jake knelt back down and laid his head against Beth's back, his tears wetting the cloth of her green dress. She wasn't moving.

He heard Williams's shuffled footsteps as he came toward them, then the words "Oh my" and "No, no" repeated in a louder and louder voice.

Williams leaned down next to Jake.

They sat in silent grief.

"Wait," Jake said, lifting his head. Williams had stopped walking, but Jake still heard footsteps.

He put his head down on Beth's back again.

They weren't footsteps. They were the beats of a heart!

"She's still alive!" Jake said.

"Jake . . ." Williams began.

"No, listen. Put your ear on her back."

Williams did. His eyes grew wide. "I'll go call for help."

Jake slid on the floor to get nearer to Beth's face. He leaned in closely and could hear breaths—laboured but definitely breaths. Then a low moan. Beth's left eye fluttered slightly open.

"Jake?" she said weakly.

"Beth."

"It hurts, Jake. It hurts." Her eyes closed again.

Jake nodded, unable to speak. He patted Beth's back as gently as he could.

Again, time seemed to move slowly.

Jake did his best to comfort his friend. He remembered something his mother had once said about keeping an injured person awake.

"Beth, stay with me."

"Jake?"

"Yes, I'm here. Don't talk."

"Don't tell me what to do," she said in a slightly stronger voice.

"Yes, boss," Jake said, smiling despite himself.

"There's something there."

"I'm sure," Jake humoured her. "Did you make it all the way up?"

Beth nodded slightly and then grunted in pain.

"I snuck in and hid when the painters were getting ready to leave. They locked the door and I climbed."

"Of course you did," Jake said.

"The drawing. The pencil lines—" She winced, and it took her a full minute to gain the strength to continue. "It's me."

"You?" Jake was sure the painters would have seen that.

"My name. It's my name."

Jake remembered that Beth had told him her father had spoken her name when he was in the hospital. It was his sign that he was ready to leave.

"My real name . . ." She went silent again.

For a horrible moment, Jake worried Beth had slipped away, then she took a breath and licked her lips. But what did she mean?

"I was so excited, I was rushing down to tell you . . ."

"And you slipped?"

Beth nodded, grunting in pain again. "Stupid leather shoes. And there was something else . . . but I can't remember now." Her eyes began to roll back.

"Beth," Jake said, "stay with me."

"Not sure I have a choice," she whispered.

The panels of the balcony slid open and Williams called down. "Help is on the way. Is Beth okay?"

Jake looked up and nodded. "I think she's got a bit of a concussion. But she's mostly making sense. So that's an improvement." Jake hoped the joke would help settle Williams's nerves, and his own.

Beth chuckled at the joke, then winced again.

Jake was sure she had a number of broken bones as well. He hoped that was all.

A siren wailed in the distance.

The sound seemed to rouse Beth. She rolled her head a bit, another good sign, and looked sideways at Jake. "Why is your hair so wet?"

Jake reached up and touched his matted curls. "Oh. I just got out of the bath."

"You took a bath in a thunderstorm?"

"Yeah."

"In water? In an electrical storm?"

"Yeah."

"And you have the nerve to call me a bonehead?"

Jake sighed. "I'll take that as a sign you're going to pull through."

Beth smiled, turned her head back to the floor, and closed her eyes. She took tiny quick breaths, wincing each time. Jake kept his hand gently on her back until the ambulance arrived to take her away.

Jake watched, feeling weak and helpless, as two men carefully lifted Beth and placed her on a cloth stretcher.

"Can I come?" he asked.

"No kids allowed," the driver said.

"Unless they're injured," Beth joked.

But Jake and Williams stayed with her as they walked out of the Regency to the waiting ambulance. She groaned slightly as the men got ready to lift her into the back of the fire-red ambulance.

Jake leaned in quickly and kissed her cheek. She whispered something only he could hear.

He stepped away as they secured the gurney and closed the ambulance doors. The siren began its high-pitched whine as the engine fired up.

As they drove away, Williams gripped Jake's shoulder. "This was all my fault. All my fault."

Jake was about to protest, but Williams held up his hand to stop him. "I'm going to send the painters home for a few days. We need to clean up and see if there's a problem with that scaffolding. But right now, I need to find Clarice and let her know what's happened."

"Clarice?"

"Beth's mother." He turned and walked back into the Regency, the doors swinging gently closed behind him.

Jake didn't tell Williams what Beth had said as he'd kissed her cheek.

"Jake, it's up there. You have to find it. Whatever it is. Promise."

CHAPTER TWENTY-FIVE

S he said she saw her name." Jake stood at the base of the scaffolding, arms crossed, legs spread wide.

Max, the head painter, looked at him like he was a stain that needed painting over, and fast. "I'm telling you, kid, there's no name. There's some rough pencil sketches—a drawing of some kind of plant, maybe. Now go away. Me and Esther gotta get back to work."

"Yeah, we're behind as it is now," Esther said. "Thanks to your little friend, we had to retighten every bolt twice."

Jake narrowed his eyes. "Maybe if you'd done that before, my 'little friend' wouldn't have slipped."

Beth had told the doctors that the pipes had begun to sway as she'd hurried down the side. The doctors had told Clarice, who'd told Williams, who'd told Jake.

Max scoffed. "Yeah, well, we weren't expecting some kid in dress shoes to sneak in and do something stupid."

Jake stared up at the scaffolding. Beth was right about the ladder rungs. One section ran up the side of the first level and ended at a floor of wooden planks. Then there was a ladder on the opposite side to reach the next set of planks, and so on until you reached the top.

Beth had fallen from about fifteen feet up, just at the top of the second ladder section. Thank goodness, because she could easily have crashed from the full height. If that had happened . . . well, Jake didn't want to think about it.

Still, Beth had a broken leg, a fractured arm, and some cracked ribs. No baseball for a while, at the very least.

Jake had offered to take her some ice cream, but apparently hospitals in Beth's time frowned on visitors, especially unaccompanied minors.

Even Beth's mom had only been allowed in a couple of times. She'd asked why Jake's mom hadn't been by to ask about Beth, and he had no good way to answer that question, so he'd been mostly hiding in his apartment.

He'd managed to track down Williams only once, practically ambushing him on his way out to deliver a package. He'd pleaded for a chance to look at the X for himself, but the architect had refused.

"No. The painters have already told us what's up there: nothing. No more falls. No more."

"But just one quick look?"

"Look, Jake, I can't make it up there. And I am certainly not allowing another child to do something so dangerous. It's over."

Since then, Williams had also been hiding away, camping out in his third-floor office. Jake had no way to get there without the key, and the Great Hall had been locked tight.

Until today, when the painters returned.

Beth had been in hospital for a few days and was due home

soon, but even then, she was also going to be stuck in bed. Not for long, if Jake knew Beth—and he did—but for a while. She certainly wouldn't be able to visit the Great Hall again before the pencil lines were painted over.

Max and his partner, Esther, went back to stirring huge pails of white paint. They had set up a pulley system to lift the paint up the scaffolding, but they mixed it first so they weren't shaking and stirring way up on top.

In a few minutes, whatever was up there, a drawing or names or whatever, was going to be covered over forever.

Everything was now in Jake's hands. Or maybe feet, he thought. Beth had slipped on the smooth metal pipes. But she'd been wearing dress shoes with slick leather soles.

Jake looked down at his own feet. He was wearing his own clothes today—grippy rubber-soled sneakers and clothes that fit—in the unlikely event the painters agreed to let him see the pencil markings for himself. He wanted zero chance of slipping or getting a loose sleeve caught on a pipe.

He stared at the ladder. The X. The scaffolding. Did he have a feeling? A conviction that Beth had seen something the painters missed?

No.

But he had promised her. Jake owed his friend, his best friend, at least that.

He took a deep breath and began climbing.

"HEY!" yelled Max.

"You've got to be kidding me," Esther said. "ANOTHER stupid kid?!"

Jake ignored them. He grabbed hold and began making his way rung by rung up the side of the tower.

Max grabbed the first rung and called up, "Get down!"

"There's something up there. And I promised." Jake turned to face Max—and instantly regretted it. He was no fan of heights. In fact, he'd never been this high off the ground. He slowed and stopped. His fingers wrapped tightly around a metal rung, but he could feel nervous sweat beginning to loosen his grip.

Max was now right behind him. "Kid, this is not some play-set. I can see you're nervous, and I'm not gonna grab you . . . but let's start climbing back down, okay?"

Jake gritted his teeth. "No. I need to see . . . for Beth." He reached for the next rung and resumed his climb, willing himself onward.

"Obnoxious little—" Max growled behind him. "Fine. Then listen to me and go slowly. When you reach the next rung, you can stand on the platform. I'll help you the rest of the way, deal?"

"Really?"

"Do I have a choice? Or are you going to do something stupid no matter what?"

"You can bet a cookie on it," Jake said. Another Beth phrase he'd picked up.

"Then really. I don't need you falling."

"Thanks."

"Don't get weepy, kid. Esther and I have three more jobs we've got to get to, and your pal's antics set us back already."

With Max's help, Jake was able to climb from platform to platform until they emerged on the highest level. Jake kept his eyes focused on the ceiling.

Max sat down on the platform to catch his breath and nod-ded toward the crossed arches. "Have a good look. I'm going to lug up the paint before I help you down. That's how long you've got to see what *isn't* there."

Now that he was up close, Jake couldn't believe how large the arches were. "Each one must have been taken from a single tree," he said.

"Yeah, yeah," Max said. "Some puzzle." He was busying himself with the rope and pulley.

Jake smiled back at the smiling face of an enormous lion just a few feet away. It was amazing how lifelike the faces appeared both from the ground and up close. Twisting vines and blossoming flowers surrounding the heads like crowns.

The effect was magical.

"Okay, satisfied?" Max was standing and motioning toward the ceiling.

"Hold on!" Jake had been so mesmerized by the carving that he hadn't even looked at the smooth wood. A part of him was hesitating in case there was nothing to see.

He walked right under the *X* and looked up. He could just reach the wood. He ran his fingers along the smooth oak. His heart was pounding, but Max was right—there was nothing.

He could see some scratch marks where Beth had tried to use her fingernails to . . . what? Carve? Crack open some secret compartment? But there were no hinges or gaps. This wood was solid.

What had she seen?

He bobbed his head from side to side and finally spotted the pencil marks the painters had seen. Already faint, they were even more faded with time. There were no words. No "Beth" written out. Just the outline of a flower.

"A flower?"

He looked from the drawing to the lion he'd been admiring just seconds before.

"The same flower."

He checked the drawing again. Yes. The same flower that Beth's father had sketched on the *X* was surrounding the majestic lion like a wreath.

It wasn't a sketch to start a new carving. It was his final message that they needed to look close by to unlock the mystery, and a clue about where to start.

Every animal head he'd seen so far was also functional, just as Beth's father had promised. So what was the lion hiding?

"Mr. Williams!" Jake called. He ran to the edge of the platform and yelled toward the balcony. "Mr. Williams!"

A hand grabbed the collar of his shirt and yanked him back. "That's WAY too close to the edge, kid. Okay, time's up. Down we go."

Jake tore himself free and ran back to the edge.

"MR. WILLIAMS!" Jake yelled one more time as Max grabbed him again and began pulling him toward the ladder.

"If he sees that I let another kid sneak up here, he's going to have my head. Let's go!"

Jake kept his eyes locked on the panels of the balcony, willing them to open.

"Now I'll go first," Max said, "but you are coming with me." He took a length of rope and tied it around Jake's waist. "In case you slip."

But it also meant that as soon as Max started descending, Jake couldn't refuse to follow.

He yelled one more time, the panic in his voice unmistakable: "JEREMIAH WILLIAMS!!!!"

Max tugged the rope and took a step toward the ladder. It was over.

Jake hung his head. He'd failed.

Then, so quiet he almost missed it, there was a click.

The panels slid apart.

Williams stood at the balcony and looked down. "Jake?" he called.

"I'm up here!" Jake yelled, waving his arms.

Williams spotted him, and he was not happy. "What the blazes? Get down from there this instant! I specifically told you not to go up that scaffolding."

"But I found it!"

Williams cocked his head. "Found what?"

Jake spat it out as quickly as he could. "The lion. The key. The flower."

"What are you talking about?"

Jake looked at Max. "Please, just one more minute."

Max debated for a second. Williams already knew Jake was on the scaffolding. That bird had flown. "Fine," he said, and began climbing back up.

Jake felt the rope slacken, and he walked back to the railing.

"The sketch is a flower. The same flower that's surrounding the lion's head up here. The same face as the lion in your office. The only one with a key. The key with an empty flowerpot. Do you understand? It all fits together."

Williams stood still, considering for a moment. Then he turned and walked back to the lion's head. He pushed the nose, and the jaw slid open. He took the silver key and walked back to the railing.

Jake nodded furiously. "I think Beth had the same idea, but she needed the key. That's where she was heading when she slipped and fell. To get the key."

"The part she didn't remember."

"I think so. But she was looking in the wrong place. There is no keyhole at the X. It's over here." He walked over and pointed straight up at the lion's head.

"I'll bring the key right down."

"No," Jake said, too eager to wait. "Throw it."

"Throw it?"

Jake smiled. "Show me that famous cannon arm."

For what seemed like the first time in ages, Williams smiled back. "Ready?"

"Definitely."

Williams reared back and tossed the key across the chasm. It seemed to follow the line of the ceiling as it made its way toward Jake.

For a second, he was worried Williams had overthrown the scaffolding, but then the key began to fall in a graceful arc.

Jake reached his hand up and snatched it. "Yes!"

"Nice catch, kid!" Max said.

"Been practising with some friends," Jake said, clutching the key to his chest. He paused for a second. If he was right, things were about to come to an end, and he had no idea what that would mean.

But the moment of hesitation passed. This wasn't about him—it was about Beth and Williams and a man he had never met who meant the world to both of them.

He walked past the X and then a few more steps to the head

183

of the lion. "Now, where are you?" he said. He ran his finger inside the mouth and felt a keyhole just at the back of the tongue.

His fingers trembled as he slipped the key into the slot . . . and turned.

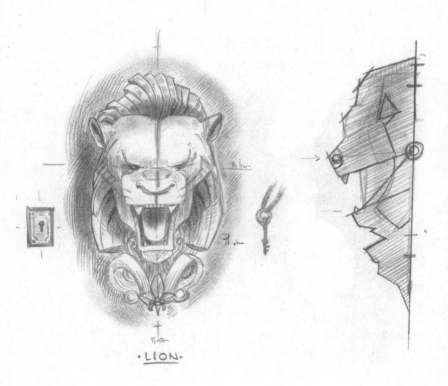

·LION·

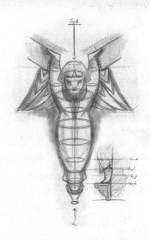

CHAPTER TWENTY-SIX

There was a click, the slow whir of gears, and a pop. Jake looked back over his shoulder. The wood right at the X had opened a crack, revealing a square-shaped gap.

Jake walked over and marvelled at the skill of the carpentry. The lines were so precisely carved they were invisible until someone used the key. Beth had scratched at the spot, sensing something was there, but even that hadn't revealed the secret.

Jake slid his fingers into the gap and pulled down gently. Spring-loaded hinges lowered a flat square of wood, and on it, a stack of leather-bound notebooks, a leather satchel, and a wooden box.

A piece of parchment paper came loose and floated down to his feet. He bent to pick it up. There was a drawing of a girl. She had the wings of an angel. Jake could make out the hint of two crossed arches behind the figure. This must have been a study for the carving that Beth's father never finished. The carving that was supposed to cover the spot where the arches crossed.

Written in a looping script along the bottom of the drawing were the words "When you are ready, open the box."

Max took off his cap and ran his fingers over his head, whistling. "Well, kid, I guess I owe you an apology."

"No need," Jake said. "That was about as well hidden as it could be." He glanced over at Williams and waved the paper. "Look!"

Williams wiped tears from his eyes and called, "I'll be there in a minute. Just need to . . . catch my breath a bit." The panels slid shut.

Jake carefully lifted the books and box off the square of wood. As he did, the box shifted slightly, revealing the cover of the top notebook. It was red, and the words "For Jeremiah" were written in gold.

Jake felt an almost overwhelming desire to turn the page, to open the box, to see what secrets lay inside. He lifted the cover, the leather resisting. Then he stopped. These were Beth's treasures, and Williams's. Not his. He felt like taking even a small peek would be stealing some of their joy at seeing the words or images for the first time. It would have been like opening Gus's boxes or Delaney's envelopes.

He closed the notebook and smiled to himself. He'd had the thrill of discovery. Sharing the next step would be sweet too.

He laid the stack carefully on the platform and used his fingers to gently push the wooden square back into place. It closed with a soft click, and the lines dissolved again into the grains of the oak.

Max signalled Esther to send up an empty bucket to safely lower the treasure to the ground. Jake helped pull it up to the top. He placed the books inside and watched them descend. His head swam a little as he realized how far up he actually was. But seeing Williams almost run from the doorway to discover what was in the bucket lifted his spirits.

"Ready for the return journey?" Max asked with a wink.

For a fleeting moment, Jake thought Max knew everything. That Jake wasn't from here. That his nebulous mission had been accomplished. Is that what he meant by the wink?

And just as he thought this, the Great Hall seemed to transform—to turn grey, dusty, its windows cracked and boarded, its golden carvings faded with time and neglect. The image seemed so real he could smell it, touch it, feel it.

Max blurred and began to melt away like a ghostly apparition.

Jake somehow knew that if he just stepped forward, he'd be home. His own home. He could almost see his mom, standing in their apartment, waiting for him.

But he didn't step forward. Should he? If he left now, would he ever see Beth again? Was she going to be okay? Would the notebooks contain anything that could help save the Regency? He gave his head a shake.

The vision began to disappear. The moment passed, and he was still here, standing on top of the platform, Williams below, and Max holding out his hand to help guide him to safety.

"So are you ready?" Max asked, a confused look on his face.

"Almost," Jake said, and he took the painter's hand and began climbing down the metal rungs one by one.

CHAPTER TWENTY-SEVEN

Beth was supposed to be in her bed, resting, letting her bones set. Recovering.

She wasn't.

"Of course," said Jake, walking into the apartment. "Surprised you're not on the field out back trying to pitch."

At the sound of his voice, Beth turned and smiled the biggest smile he had ever seen.

"JAKE!"

Beth hobbled toward him, her good arm resting on a wooden crutch for balance. Her head was bandaged and bruised, but she was clearly going to be okay. His heart swelled.

Before she could reach him, the looming shadow of Mrs. Matthewson suddenly appeared between them.

"If you're here to try talking my daughter into more irresponsible, reckless, *dangerous*—" She stopped, her lips trembling. "She could have died, Jake."

Jake nodded. "I know. And if I had been there—"

"A fine pair of detectives! Planning this escapade together!"

Jake sputtered. "But . . . but . . ."

"And now Jeremiah tells me *you* pulled the same stunt?! What is wrong with kids today? When I see your mother, we'll have a lot to talk about."

Before Jake could say another word, Mrs. Matthewson reached out and buried him in a giant hug.

Beth's head popped up over her back as Jake felt the air leave his lungs. "Nice work there, bucko," she said. She held up the green notebook he had found in the ceiling. Williams had delivered the precious books, which is how Jake had found out Beth was indeed home.

He still had no idea what was inside any of them.

Beth's mom released Jake and used her apron to wipe a tear from her eye. "Now, I've got a special dinner planned, so I need to get back to work." She smiled and disappeared into the kitchen.

"Please don't say it," Jake said.

"Aspic." Beth smiled. "Your favourite." Then she leapt toward Jake and hugged him. "Thank you so much. So, so much."

"You're hurt!" Jake said, hugging Beth back as gingerly as he could manage.

"Slightly damaged. I'll be back up and good as new in a few days." But she winced in pain as she leaned back on the crutch.

Jake led her to the dining room.

Beth held the notebook tightly in her good arm.

"So what's inside?"

Her eyes began to water. "My father's sketches. And instructions. And more. A lot of it is personal."

Jake nodded. "And the box was filled with his carving tools?" he guessed.

189

"Yes. Mine now. I'm going to finish what he started. Once I've had some practice."

"I don't doubt it."

"I've already done some carving." She leaned in close to whisper in Jake's ear. "My bedpost. Don't tell Mother."

"Shouldn't you be resting?"

"Humph. I might look broken, but I feel whole again. Thanks to you, Jake."

"I just finished what *you* started," he said. He placed his hand on hers and gave a gentle squeeze. They sat quietly for a few minutes, just smiling at each other.

"So now that you have your buried treasure, what next?" Jake asked.

"Well, I obviously need to practise a lot. But I think I'll ask Mr. Williams if I can finish the carving where Father stopped. He's already agreed to put off the painting."

Jake chuckled. "Poor Max and Esther. They're never going to want to work here again."

"They'll just have to come back and add gold to the beautiful angel I'm going to carve."

She opened the notebook and showed Jake the drawings her father had left behind. She'd added even more flowers and vines to the design.

"Those are the same flowers that your dad carved around the lion. The one he had sketched on the wood."

Beth smiled as she carefully turned the pages. "Lilies. That's how I knew where he wanted me to look."

Jake was confused. "But I thought you told Mr. Williams that you saw your name up there?"

Beth nodded. "I did."

"But it was just the drawing of a flower."

Beth sniffed and nodded again, slowly. "My name."

"Your name is Beth."

She shook her head. "That's only part. You see"—she paused—"my father was the only one who ever called me by my full name. That's how I knew he was better at the hospital. When he used my full name to call to me. And when he died, I refused to let anyone else use that name."

Jake hesitated, but he had to ask. "So your real name isn't Beth?"

"Yes and no. My full name is Lilibeth. Lily. That's what my father called me: Lily. You gave that back to me too, Jake. I want to be called Lily again."

Jake's fingertips trembled. "Lilibeth. Beth, Lily. But . . . but that's impossible."

Beth stared at him, her brow furrowed. "Don't spoil the moment, bonehead," she said. Then she smiled. "Cat got your tongue? I know how much you like cats."

But Jake's mind was spinning. Lily? His Lily? That was impossible. His mind went back to the torn and burned photo on Lily's mantel. The man, faded and blurred. Her father. The faded drawings on her walls of flowers and animals. His and hers.

His fate had always been tied to hers. And hers to the Regency.

The room began to spin. Actually spin. The walls seemed to fly away into darkness. He had the same feeling he'd had on the scaffolding after finding the notebooks. But this time, instead of taking a step forward, he could feel some force pulling him back.

Mrs. Matthewson called from the kitchen. "You're staying for dinner, right, Jake? Jeremiah is coming as well. Lily and I have a lot to celebrate."

But now Jake could see it. Apartment 713 was dissolving. He fought the pull, part of him not sure he wanted to leave at all.

He reached out his hand to Beth. "Come with me?"

She arched an eyebrow. "Where?" She nodded toward the crutch that she was leaning on. "I'm not exactly up for a big trip."

"I can feel it. I'm leaving."

"Feel . . . what? Leave for where?"

"Whatever the Regency wanted, it's done. I'm going home." He wanted to laugh and cry at the same time. He didn't want to say goodbye.

Beth took his hand and scanned his face. "I don't know, Jake. I . . . my mother."

"She can come too. She *should* come! All the amazing people you can meet. Delaney, Gus . . . Oh no! I need to get their gifts."

Jake stood up straight, releasing Beth's hand. "I'll run. I just need to grab the stuff I collected for everyone." He hurried to the door and turned.

Beth had followed him to the entrance. She leaned on her crutch and smiled at him. She was all he could see clearly now as the apartment seemed to swim and swirl around her.

"I'll be right back," Jake said. "I promise."

"I'll wait for you," she said. "I promise."

He turned the handle, opened the door, and stepped into the hallway.

The door slammed behind him.

A set of keys jingled in the lock.

CHAPTER TWENTY-EIGHT

J ake froze. The keys swung and jangled against each other behind him, ticking like an old clock winding down.

Jake looked down at his feet. The carpet was worn, the wood slats underneath stained and gouged. The lights in the aged sconces flickered and dimmed.

He was home. Home home. The Regency, but in the future. And he was alone.

"Beth?" he said, turning around. He pulled at the handle, but the door to apartment 713 stayed shut. He knocked his fist against the wood and yelled through the door.

"BETH! LILY!"

Jake pressed his ear against the door but heard nothing from the other side.

He turned the keys, but they just spun and spun in the lock. The door stayed shut.

Jake leaned his head against the hard wood. His heart was racing.

He'd left Beth behind. She was gone.

He'd gone to get his stupid gifts. He should have stayed with her. He should have convinced her to come with him.

The small flame of joy he felt at being home was swallowed in a swirl of sadness.

"I should be happy, right?" he whispered. Then he gently bumped the door with his forehead, the sound swallowed up by the dusty air of the hallway.

"Jake?" The deep voice was coming from somewhere down the hallway.

Jake turned his head slowly, his forehead still against the door. "Mr. Williams?"

"Mr. Williams? Jake, you feeling okay?"

"Danny?" Jake pushed himself upright. "Is that really you?"

He made a show of checking his name tag. "Apparently."

"Danny, I'm so sorry. You must have been worried."

"About leaving my keys?"

Jake shook his head. "No. Um . . . keys?" He had to think back to remember what Danny was talking about. It seemed so long ago. The morning he'd disappeared, he'd had the keys only because Danny had left them behind. Jake had totally forgotten that. How did Danny even remember?

"Wasn't that, like, weeks ago?"

"More like thirty minutes," Danny said. "Maybe a few more."

Jake closed his eyes. "No. No. Thirty minutes? I've been gone for weeks."

"Gone? Weeks?" Danny walked over and put the back of his hand on Jake's forehead. "You feel a little hot. Maybe you need to sit down?"

Jake shook him off. "No, it's true. The light for 713 lit up. You forgot your keys."

"That's why I've been looking for you. I knocked on your door. No answer. Your mom left for that interview, I guess."

"Interview," Jake repeated. "So my mom never even knew I was gone?"

"Well, like I said, there was no one at your place. I'm not sure there was any reason to worry about you."

"And you couldn't find me because I was in there." Jake pointed at the number on the door.

"In . . . *there?*"

"Yeah. I unlocked the door, but then it locked behind me. I got trapped. In the past."

"Uh-huh." Danny was clearly not buying this.

"I was there for at least a month. I just stepped back out."

Danny chuckled. "I told you, you can't go in there."

"I know. And I'm sorry, but—"

Danny interrupted him. "No. I didn't mean you can't, like it's not allowed. I meant you can't go in there because . . . well, try to open the door again."

Jake turned the keys. They spun, but the lock still refused to click open. "But I was just IN there."

"Not sure how that's possible. There was a fire in there, years and years ago. It's been closed off ever since. At least that's the story. Another mystery."

"Fire?" Jake gave his head another shake. "No. I'm telling you I was just in there, Danny. Jeremiah Williams is there. Beth is in there. I was just talking to her."

"Beth?"

"That's what I called her. But it was Lily! Our Lily! When she was a kid." He was bursting to share everything with Danny, but then the superintendent winced as if he'd been hit.

"What's wrong?" Jake asked.

"Jake, Lily is . . ." Danny ran his fingers over his chin, clearly trying to say something important and not sure how. He avoided Jake's eyes.

Jake's heart raced. "Lily is *what*, Danny?"

"The call I got *was* from Delaney. He'd found Lily. She'd been wandering the hallways. She collapsed."

"Collapsed?"

"The ambulance guys are there now—"

Jake didn't wait to hear the rest. He bolted to the stairs and slammed open the door. He'd just lost the Beth from the past. Now was he going to lose her forever?

He leapt down the stairs five at a time, holding on to the wooden railings as he swung himself around each corner.

Even before he got to the door to the fourth floor, he heard the murmur of concerned voices.

He took a deep breath and opened the door as quickly and quietly as he could. Two ambulance attendants were standing on either side of a metal gurney, fiddling with a web of tubes and wires. They turned to face him.

One held a finger to her lips. "Shhhh." She inclined her head toward the gurney, which looked empty.

Jake swallowed the lump in his throat and walked quietly toward them.

It wasn't empty. Lily was so thin she was barely visible under the large blue blanket. She looked even more frail than Jake remembered. She was perfectly still. Her eyes were closed.

"Is she . . . ?" Jake asked.

"She's very weak," the attendant said. "We were just about to get her to the hospital. But then these stupid cats surrounded the gurney and we had to shoo them back into the apartment first."

Jake could hear mewing from the other side of Lily's door. If the cats hadn't done that, he'd have missed her completely. "Thanks, guys," he said.

A whisper from the gurney drew his attention back.

Lily was looking up at him, a thin smile on her lips.

"Jake?"

He was too shocked to answer. He nodded silently and leaned closer.

"You're here." Her eyes narrowed and locked on his face. The confusion he'd seen there so often before seemed to flicker away. "I waited, Jake. I told you I would. I promised." She beamed.

Tears filled Jake's eyes. Lily remembered? How was that possible?

"Lily," he said. "Beth."

"Be happy, Jake." She reached a hand to his face and wiped away a tear. The effort was draining, and her hand fell back to the blanket.

Jake reached out and took it in his, gently squeezing her fingers. Her skin felt like paper. "I just saw you. I was just there with you."

Lily smiled. "The aspic was delicious." She winked.

"I doubt that," Jake laughed, but he also choked back a sob.

"Don't forget to get outside more. And work on hitting that fastball." He saw a flash of a young Lily, of Beth, in her eyes and her mischievous smile. "Look behind the lily. Goodbye, Jake."

Then, in an instant, like a cloud obscuring the sun, it was gone. Lily looked at Jake as if he'd just arrived.

"Steve?" she said. "Thank you for coming. Anastasia will be so pleased."

"No, no. It's me, Jake. Beth, it's me."

"Beth?" She smiled. "No one has called me that in a long, long time."

"I miss you," Jake said. "Please don't go."

But Beth was gone.

"Anastasia is so hungry, Steve," Lily said. Her head rolled back onto the pillow, and she stared up for a moment before closing her eyes again. Her hand went limp in his.

"Beth?" Jake said. "Lily? Beth?"

The attendants pushed Jake gently aside and began adjusting the tubes and wires again.

"We've got to get her to the hospital," one of them said.

But Jake could tell the urgency was missing from his voice.

Jake leaned against the wall and watched them hoist the gurney and wheel it carefully down the hallway to the service elevator. He followed in a daze. Only a few days before, he'd seen Beth carried away in an ambulance. She had come back. He knew Lily wasn't going to.

The doors slid apart. Danny was there, holding the elevator open until the gurney was safely inside.

"I'm sorry. No kids allowed," said the woman.

"I'm coming," Jake said, stepping forward. He hadn't been allowed to see Beth in hospital, and he was determined to stay with Lily.

Danny put a hand on his shoulder. "You can't help, Jake. But Lily needs you to do something else." He pointed over the boy's shoulder.

Jake turned. Anastasia the kitten was bounding down the

hallway carpet toward the elevator. The other cats peeked their heads out of the doorway.

"We've got to go," the woman said.

Jake took one look back at Lily and knew she was gone.

He'd lost her again.

But Danny was right—there was something left for him to do. Something she would have wanted him to do.

Jake stepped back into the hallway. He knelt down and scooped up Anastasia, who nuzzled his cheek with her soft fur.

Danny gave Jake a weak smile and pushed the button for the lobby.

The elevator doors slid closed. Jake stood staring at the panels, listening to the whirring of the cables as they took Lily—Beth—away.

CHAPTER TWENTY-NINE

J̲ake hugged Anastasia to his chest, his heart breaking. Beth *had* waited. She'd promised Jake she would, and she had. He couldn't believe it. Then again, knowing Beth, she had probably just willed herself to stay alive until he returned.

But what had he achieved by going back to her time? By coming back now? By having such a short time to say goodbye?

Had they saved the Regency? He snorted. It still looked run-down, falling apart, and was no doubt about to be demolished.

And his best friend was gone forever. For what?

Anger mixed with sadness and confusion, and shook him. "Why? Why?" he yelled at the walls. "What was the stupid point of all this?"

Jake's ear tingled.

"Anastasia, stop," he said. But Anastasia, startled by his shouting, had jumped back down to the carpet and was walking to the apartment.

The stairway door fluttered open a crack, and there was a soft whistle of wind. It brushed against his cheek.

He spun, expecting to see Beth standing next to him. He could almost swear that he'd felt her breath.

"Beth?" He shook his head. "Beth?" But he was alone.

Anastasia gave a petulant meow from the open doorway. She strutted inside, and Jake heard the telltale scrape of the empty food bowl being slid on the tile floor. He waited for a minute more, then hung his head and walked to Lily's apartment.

He slowly pushed aside the door and realized with a start that he had been there just a day before. He'd made tea for Lily. The cups sat in the middle of the table. The empty food dish sat between the legs of Lily's chair. The cans of cat food that Jake himself had opened and rinsed were in a bag by the sink. He opened some new cans and refilled the bowl. The cats dove hungrily at the jiggling meal.

"Looks like veal aspic," Jake said with a laugh. "Who's going to take care of you cats now?"

They didn't answer.

He stood up and looked around.

The apartment was slightly different than he remembered. The pictures on the mantel drew him over. The family photos seemed brighter. The people were the same, but were the smiles wider? No, they were posing in a different place. Outside, in front of a beautiful mural. A mural of flowers in sunlight.

And there were framed photos he was sure he hadn't seen before. A picture of Lily and Georgia! They were on horseback in front of a cactus-covered hill.

There was a picture of Lily, her face shining with a glorious smile, posing in an airplane cockpit. She was dressed in goggles and a leather hat and coat.

Lily in a skirt, throwing a baseball.

Lily in a wedding dress with a dapper-looking man.

And there were more framed drawings on the wall. Jake choked up as he realized they were signed "Lilibeth Matthewson."

Then, on the slightly-less-faded ones, "Lilibeth Gibson."

Lilibeth had grown up and had a life, a good life. A life Jake was now seeing in glimpses. A life that, maybe, he had helped make a little better? That thought, finally, cheered him.

"You did it, Beth," Jake said as he admired a photo of a teenage Lily posing on scaffolding alongside a delicately carved angel. "Beautiful."

Beth had taken her father's lessons to heart.

Jake lifted the frame.

Was this the "lily" he was supposed to look behind? Or was he supposed to look behind the actual carving? He doubted Danny would let him climb up to see.

He put the frame down and looked more closely at the drawings on the wall.

His eyes immediately went to the drawing of the angel that Beth had shown him, the one she'd turned into the final carving. The one her father had begun and she'd finished.

The edges of the paper were slightly singed.

He peered at the signature. "Lily 'Beth' Gibson."

"Of course," he chuckled. There were many "Lilibeth's" on the wall, but only one "Lily." He took the frame down gently. Anastasia was back, curling around his feet, purring, her tiny tail twitching.

Jake turned the frame around and placed it face down on the kitchen table. An envelope was taped to the back. "For Jake" was written across it in a faltering hand.

He opened it, and out dropped a key. But not any key.

Jake picked it up and felt an electric charge run through his arm. He knew this key very well.

He petted Anastasia gently. "I'll be back soon. And I promise I'll take care of you."

He stood up, clutching the key tightly in his hand.

He closed the apartment door carefully behind him, making sure all the cats were safely inside, and walked briskly toward the elevator.

CHAPTER THIRTY

J ake held the key against the cracked button for the third
floor and paused. Would it still work? Was the crack filled
with decades of dust and grit?

He took a deep breath and slid the key inside. It clicked as if
it were brand new. The elevator began to descend, slowly, creak-
ing and lurching. "If Mr. Williams could hear this racket, he'd
have a fit," Jake said to his infinite reflections.

Then he remembered that Williams would have died years
before. Jake missed him. Everything had happened so fast that
he never got a chance to say goodbye.

The elevator stopped at the third floor. The iron gate slid
aside. The panels groaned and creaked, shuddering as they tried
to open. Then the gate began to close.

"Oh no, you don't," Jake said.

He jammed his foot against the gate then wedged his fingers
into the gap between the panels. He leaned to his right, using his
body weight to force the doors apart.

They groaned and creaked and then finally lurched open. Jake leapt past them and inside the balcony.

The elevator doors closed behind him, throwing him into complete darkness.

"You never make anything easy, do you, Beth?" He flicked the light switch in the pillar, but the lights did not turn on. Feeling along the walls, he made his way around the office. His hand triggered the jaw of the lion, and he heard it open with a screech of metal.

"I'll deal with you in a minute," he said.

Finally, he reached his target: the edge of the balcony. Even without seeing, he could feel that the oak railing was rougher, more worn, and more nicked than the last time he'd touched it. He could almost see Williams standing there, looking down on another amazing performance.

Jake reached out and grabbed the bear's paw. Although slightly tougher to pull, it moved. The panels of the outside wall began to shift aside, stuttering slightly in their rails from years of disuse, but disappearing into the side walls nevertheless.

A greyish light, so diluted Jake barely had to wait before his eyes adjusted, spread across the office. The sight left him both awed and saddened. The Great Hall was filled with crates, boxes, broken remnants of chairs and tables, scraps of wood and torn curtains. Everything was covered in a thick layer of dust.

It looked more like a garbage dump than the heart of a grand building. The windows were papered over or boarded up with plywood. Only slivers of light crept through where the paper had dried and split, barely offering enough light to see.

"Cleaning this place is going to be job number one," Jake

said. "If I get the chance." The X was in shadow, but Jake was sure he could see the outline of a figure staring back at him. "Actually, getting the lights back on is job number one." He couldn't wait to see the carving.

He turned back to the office. The velvet seat of the chair looked like it had been chewed on by an animal—one Jake really hoped wasn't lurking somewhere in the shadows. Williams's elegant desk was more worn along the edges, and the green leather of the desk pad was cracked and dry.

Jake sat down, releasing a puff of dust. He coughed and waved the air in front of his face. "So, Beth, what am I looking for?"

He searched the desktop, lifting the pad, parts of which dissolved at his touch, and found nothing. A silver letter opener and a few nubs of pencils rolled along the empty bottom of a side drawer, but that was it.

He sat back in the chair and looked over at the lion. Its mouth hung open, and lying on the red velvet tongue was a key. But not the key that had been there before—the one he'd used to open the X in Beth's time.

This key was smaller.

Jake walked over. He reached inside and took the key. He held it up. The handle was embossed with the face of a smiling puppy.

Jake smiled and looked at the puppy Beth's father had carved into the wall. It sat above one of the many unopened drawers. Or at least they had been unopened when Jake had last set foot in the office.

He pulled the chair over and climbed up on it, balancing on the handles. Although the leather had become fragile, the chair itself was still sturdy. "Nice work, Mr. Matthewson," he said as he reached up and slipped the key into the hole under the puppy's head.

There was a click and the drawer slid open. "Yes!" Jake reached over the side and felt around. He pulled out a small envelope with his name written on it in the same wobbly hand he'd seen behind the drawing. There was also another key.

He felt around to make sure he hadn't left anything behind, and his finger rubbed against the smooth leather and coarse stitching of a baseball. "No way," Jake said. He rolled the ball with his fingertips to the end of the drawer and eased it over the edge.

He stared in wonder at the inscription—"To Gus"—and the unmistakable signatures of Babe Ruth and Cool Papa Bell.

The ball had browned a bit with age and the ink had faded slightly, but when Jake held it to his nose and took a deep breath, it smelled like the lot behind the Regency on a sunny afternoon.

"Thank you, Beth," he said.

He sat back down, then took the silver letter opener and carefully slid it under the flap of the envelope. The note inside was written in a steadier hand than the first one he'd found. The paper seemed older, more brittle.

He had to pause more than once as he read.

Dear Jake,

When you didn't come back right away, I was hurt. But that passed. You had promised me you'd be back, and I knew you meant it, so I knew something else must have happened. It was only then that I truly accepted what you had told me repeatedly—that you were not from my time.

Please forgive my skepticism. But also, to be fair, you are a weirdo, so it's not all my fault.

Jake chuckled. He could hear her voice, as clearly as if she were reading the letter to him.

Mr. Williams looked for you everywhere. I told him you had been called home. He was confused, and I wasn't sure how much to tell him. But he kept your apartment free, in case you returned. He was very fond of you, Jake.

When I saw that the treasures you'd collected were still there, untouched under the closet floorboards, I knew you'd be worried. Gus, Delaney, and the others must mean a lot to you. I hope to meet them someday. And I know you'd want them to have these gifts. So they are safely in my apartment, under my bed.

"But then why are you here?" Jake asked the baseball. The baseball stayed silent.

I think I know why you were sent home. The more I think about what we did—finding my father's notebooks hidden at the very centre, the heart, of this wonderful building—the more I believe our futures hinged on that. Yours. Mine. Maybe the future of the Regency as well? I still don't know.

Maybe Mr. Williams is right. Maybe the Regency isn't meant to last forever. But if his ideas—ideas my father shared in his writing—live on, then we have made the world a better place.

You see, what we found in the X was more than just a collection of drawings and notes. So much more.

Father poured his heart and his soul into the pages. Just

as he'd poured them into the building while he was able to work. He knew he was dying—how could he not?—and he wanted to share what was left of his vision, his skills, and more personal things. Things he wrote to me, to Mother, and to Mr. Williams.

Without you, I never would have even begun to search. You did that, Jake. I cannot thank you enough, and I know, someday, we will meet again. I cannot wait for that as well.

Jake read the letter over and over, choking up each time. He set it aside and rolled the baseball in his fingers. Then he tossed it up in the air and caught it.

What was it doing here? Where were the other treasures? Beth had written so much but left so much unanswered.

He put the ball down and picked up the new key. The handle was shaped into the face of a wild boar.

Jake looked at the wall. A boar stared back from just above the floor-boards.

He walked over, knelt down, and opened the drawer.

CHAPTER THIRTY-ONE

J ake reached inside and pulled out another envelope and another key. And rolled up like parchment, the record sleeve with the words "Best wishes to a real cracker*jake*. Louis Armstrong."

The edges of the brittle paper were slightly charred. He set the sleeve carefully on top of the desk and opened the envelope. Another letter in a stronger hand, older.

> *It has taken me years to be able to write this down, and even now, it makes my heart break in so many ways. You've seen the burned edge of the record sleeve.*
>
> *There was a fire.*
>
> *Caused by? Who knows? I was outside playing baseball when I heard the glass in the window shatter. I saw immediately that it was our apartment, and I ran.*
>
> *Mr. Williams had pulled Mother from the fire, but she had breathed in too much smoke.*

The words swam as Jake read.

> *... ran back ... father's drawings ...*
> *... The gifts were in a trunk. I pulled it out from under ...*
> *Mr. Williams called me a fool for running back into the fire.*
> *I believe you would have used the term "bonehead." I have always been both and remain proud of it. Ha! At least my boneheadedness helped me save some precious memories.*
> *But not my mother.*

Jake shook his head, amazed yet again at his friend's ability to find a laugh in the middle of such sadness.

> *Mr. Williams adopted me. He supported my artistic endeavours, and even sent me to art school. No floor cleaning for me!*
> *And as a companion, he gifted me a cat. I named her Petunia, after the girl in the pirate radio show that was on when we first met. I still don't know if that girl escaped. As far as I know, she is still trapped in that cave, menaced by pirates for all eternity.*
> *Maybe you can go back in time and save her too!*
> *You were right about cats. They are wonderful and strange creatures. And unlike you, this one loves aspic. I think I might get another. There are always strays around. If I find a particularly scruffy and lost-looking one, I'll name him Jake.*
> *P.S. To be honest, I think Mr. Williams believes that mice may have caused the fire, and he gave me Petunia to guard against future disaster.*

There were more keys, more letters, and more precious artifacts of Jake's own brief time in the past: the movie poster, the biscotti recipe, and the notes from Albert Einstein.

In one letter, Beth wrote that she was giving Jake a taste of the fun she and Mr. Williams had when they—finally—opened all the doors.

And there was one note that made Jake's head ache.

A surprise twist! A man with your last name came to us in desperation, a young family in tow. Mr. Williams saw this as an omen and gave him the keys to apartment 901. It was the last vacancy, and I don't know where he would have gone otherwise.

Jake took a second to let that sink in. His great-grandfather had been in the Regency. He'd had an apartment because Jake had had the apartment and Williams had kept it waiting for him. But Jake had been in that apartment only because his family was there first. His brain hurt trying to figure it all out.

There was bad news, and although Jake knew it was coming, it still hurt.

The stock market crash had wiped out Williams's savings. He was forced to sign the deal with the city.

A few years later, he died.

Beth struggled to make the building work.

The Regency, while battered and aged, still seems noble. But it is getting harder and harder to keep the place as it should be. Like a ship that springs two holes for each one we repair. We've had to close some of the apartments. Maybe the Regency won't even survive until you return. Maybe I am writing you these letters in vain.

Bit by bit, note by note, Jake was able to piece together his friend's life since he'd disappeared. Sometimes years passed between notes, but she had continued to try to tell him her story.

Jake, I wrote years ago about holes in a sinking ship. The holes are still there, but I know that the Regency will continue to float until you arrive. I am sure of it. And you know me—I'm always right!

I am enclosing some trifles that I hope will help as you fight to save this beautiful building. I tried to remember some of the items that you said still existed in your time— soda drinks and chocolate bars—so I bought some stock in a few companies.

Of course, I've had to sell many shares along the way— for my family, and for those many holes I mentioned—but perhaps what's left will be of use after I am gone.

Jake took a second, exhaling deeply.

And I have also enclosed a journal I kept over the years of people who have passed through these walls. People who might be able to help?

A large envelope contained stock certificates for companies that even Jake had heard of. Not a lot. But some. How much would they be worth? Jake wasn't sure. Enough to save a building? He doubted that. But maybe enough to *help* save one. She'd at least left him a chance.

There was a thin notebook in the envelope with the names and addresses of people Jake assumed were famous, or had been. *I'll google them*, he thought, then couldn't help but laugh out loud.

And there was one final key that revealed one final letter.

The hand that wrote the words was uneven, the words shaky and hard to read. But Jake gripped the paper tighter and tighter as he read.

My memories are fading, Jake. They come to me in flashes, but when I try to reach out and hold them, they run through my fingers like mist.

I am so old. Too old, I fear, to believe that we will meet again. I now wish I had told you more, left you more, as the things I'd hoped to say to you in person begin to fly away like dust in the last rays of daylight.

But I have lived a full and busy life. I have been surrounded by love, by art, by cats—all in a home that has a heart. Perhaps what I have told you and left you is enough? You gave me the gift of hope, and I have to believe that I have passed some of that hope back to you.

You never told me what my future would be, and I think that was for the best. It might not even be the same as the future you saw before we met. Who can say?

I do know that I have never stopped missing you.

Your (Lily) Beth

Jake sat back in the chair. He held the letter to his chest. Tears filled his eyes. He felt such a strange collection of emotions—sadness, exhaustion, but also happiness.

And hope. He did feel hope.

Beth had given that to him.

Yes, she had left him some money.

But she'd also left a book filled with people who could help tell the story of the building. He could tell that story too.

The story of a great architect and a great artist who came together to build a beautiful place around a beautiful idea. And another great artist who had carried on that legacy.

They had been lost to time, and they should not have been. He would make sure they weren't anymore.

Would it work? He didn't know.

Was it worth trying? Maybe.

Was he going to try?

Jake knew the answer to that last question, and he said it loud.

"YES!"

CHAPTER THIRTY-TWO

J ake sat on the end of his bed, waiting for his mother to come home, amazed at how strangely time can bend and twist.

He'd been gone for weeks—which turned out to be minutes—and had just arrived home. And yet, in that short or long time, his whole universe had been turned upside down.

Then his first day back had seemed to stretch to give him an impossible amount of time to start putting his plan—*their* plan—into action.

First, he'd given Danny the notebook. Danny did know a lot of the names Lily had written down. Artists, musicians, actors—exactly the sort of people who would step up to save the Regency.

"I'll start calling first thing tomorrow," Danny said.

"Be nice to see the Great Hall filled with some great performances again."

"*Again*? How do you know about the Great Hall?"

Jake shrugged. "I'm like the Regency. Filled with secrets." He had decided to keep the full story to himself . . . for now.

"Hey, Danny, do you know any reporters who might want to take a closer look at the story of this place?"

"Actually, I do. There were a few who stayed here a while back, after Lily stopped updating her book. Definitely worth a few calls."

"I can see the newsies on the corner yelling out the headline already: 'Local Kid Discovers the Latest Wonder of the World—Right Here in Our City!'"

"Newsies?"

Danny's phone had rung before Jake could explain. It was Lily's family calling from the hospital. But Jake already knew that Lily was gone. Still, the finality of the news had hurt. A lot.

Danny looked deflated as he put the phone back in its cradle.

Jake walked over and gave the giant man a giant hug. "She isn't gone," he said. "She's here. Everywhere. And we're not going to let anyone tear that down."

"We can fight city hall after all," Danny said, wiping a tear away.

That conversation felt as if it had happened ages ago, and yet the setting sun was still gleaming through his window. Dust particles danced in the golden beams.

Anastasia walked through the rays, creating swirling graceful arcs in the dust. They reminded Jake of the vines he'd seen carved throughout the Regency.

The kitten picked at the loose flap of wallpaper.

"Stop that," Jake said. "I already feel bad enough about wrecking the painting without you making it worse."

He reached down to pick her up and stared at the wooden

slats peeking out from behind the scrap. "Now I have to glue it again."

Anastasia meowed and scratched her back against the corner of the wall.

Jake cocked his head. Something wasn't right. Something about the wall itself. He stood up and began walking, one foot placed against the other, along the length of the wall.

He'd spent days lying on this floor, right where his bed was now, watching as Georgia had transformed the wall into a beautiful cityscape. And he was sure this wall was now a full six inches longer and wider.

Why?

He got down on his knees and squinted, peering into the darkness between the slats. As his eyes adjusted, he could see the lights of a skyscraper staring back through wisps of city smoke.

He jammed his fingers between the wooden slats and pulled. At first, the thin wood refused to budge, but soon the ancient nails gave up their grip on the studs and an entire section of wall swung away as if it were on hinges.

Jake stared at the hole in amazement.

Georgia's mural was still there, almost as brilliant as the day she'd finished it. The Regency, bathed in silver light, rose into the sky like a noble giant.

Someone—possibly his grandfather, possibly Williams or Lily—had protected the mural by hiding it behind a false wall. He didn't know why, but he thanked them just the same.

Jake was sure the other apartments on the ninth floor would yield equally spectacular secrets. Maybe a mural painted by Lily? He was sure of it.

"Wow, Anastasia. Wow!"

There was a thump as something hit the floor.

"JAKE! WHAT IN THE NAME OF?!!"

His mother was standing in the doorway, shocked and shaking. A bag of groceries lay open at her feet, a dozen oranges rolling around on the floor.

Anastasia walked over and began playing with them.

"Mom!" He wanted to jump up, hug her, tell her how much he missed her. But the look on her face—jaw open, eyes shaking—kept him rooted to the spot.

Jake followed her eyes to the rubble of wooden slats and plaster. It did not look good.

"I can explain."

But his mother had walked into the room. She pointed at the wall.

"Is that a Georgia O'Keeffe poster?"

"O'Keeffe? Is that her last name?"

His mom walked right up and peered at the haloed top of the Regency. "This is a . . . painting! An actual Georgia O'Keeffe painting!"

Now Jake hugged her, wrapping his arms tightly around her waist. "I missed you, Mom."

She ran her fingers through his hair. "Well, you'd better get used to it, kiddo." She stared at him and smiled, her eyebrows wiggling.

"You got the job?"

"I got the job! I got it!"

He hugged her again.

"Maybe, if I can save up some money again, we can find a nicer home."

Jake looked up at his mom, tears in his eyes. "Mom, this is our home."

She turned and swallowed him in her arms.

The good news only made the hug feel warmer.

EPILOGUE

Jake was delivering the last of the presents when his phone buzzed. A text from his mom that she would be home late again.

"Sorry, Jake. Past month has been packed."

"Overtime!" Jake texted back. "I've got dinner. <3"

He put the phone back in his pocket. When they'd first moved to the Regency, he had to give his old one up. He'd been angry about that. But while hanging with Beth, he'd gotten used to being without one. There was a kind of freedom in not having something nagging at him all day long.

He had Anastasia the kitten for that.

But the calls had been coming in from Danny's reporter friends, and even some reporters Danny didn't know, and Jake wasn't going to miss one of those for the world.

He looked at his list of gifts. Most had been checked off.

Jake had given Delaney the recipe for biscotti and a few others that Lilibeth had collected over the years. Delaney had immediately begun organizing ingredients to try the recipe and add his own variations. The brown cat Delaney had agreed to take care of, Molasses, seemed equally delighted.

Jake delivered the record sleeve to Theo, who had run his fingers across the delicate signature again and again, then sat back down at the piano and composed a song on the spot. His new orange tabby, Satchmo, waved his tail in time with the song from the top of the piano.

The Professor didn't react when he laid the Einstein formula on her laptop. But he heard her gasp as he was cleaning up the kitchen. Jake hadn't asked her to take care of one of the cats, but somehow a black-and-white one named Nova had crept into the apartment. He made sure she got some of the nightly delivery of chicken and rice.

The "vintage" wig he'd given Javier elicited a happy shriek that Jake was sure scared the pigeons off the nearby rooftops. It certainly gave Javier's new furry pal, Divine, a fright.

And Jake had finally met Gus face to face. He'd passed the ball to him through the crack in the door. Gus was so amazed he'd opened the door. He wore a patch over one of his eyes, and part of his face was covered with burn marks and scars.

"You have got to be kidding me," he said in his rasping voice. He held the ball in both palms as if it were a glass egg that might shatter. "Is this real?"

Jake nodded. "There's even a letter from Lily that proves it." He had come up with the story that Lily had left these gifts to everyone in her will. "She says you are free to do anything you want with it. Sell it. Keep it. Play baseball with it."

"I'm not selling this or playing catch," Gus said. He shook his head, mesmerized. "Do you know what Cool Papa's stats were?"

"I bet you do."

"A .336 average. Fourteen doubles, seven homers, and a .517 slugging percentage."

"Amazing."

Jake decided to press his luck. "Hey, Gus," he said, "you ever want to play catch sometime?"

Gus began to close the door. "I don't like crowds."

"I get that. No need to go outside. There's a huge room I know of on the second floor where we could play catch. Or even just here in the hallway."

Gus let the door sway open again. "Seriously?"

Jake nodded. "Maybe tomorrow, before the game starts on the radio?"

"Yeah. Maybe tomorrow." Gus walked back inside, his door closing slowly behind him. Jake heard the soft mewing of Satchel just as the door clicked shut.

Jake remembered with a start that the only glove he owned was the ancient one he'd used way back when. Lily had left it for him in one of the drawers, and the leather was as thin as ever. *Maybe I can borrow a work glove from Danny to fit inside?* he thought.

He hoped Gus wasn't a fireball pitcher, but he suspected he might be.

The final gift? That was meant for Danny. It was the key to the secret third-floor office.

"I didn't even know this was here," Danny had said as they'd stepped onto the marble tiles. Jeremiah the cat had followed them from the basement and leapt onto the desktop, tail swishing.

"I feel like the superintendent of such a lovely place should have a nicer spot to eat lunch than a dingy old basement," Jake said. Then he walked over and pulled the bear's paw, watching Danny's eyes grow even wider. He stared in wonder at the view from the open balcony as Jeremiah paced along the oak railing like a tightrope walker.

Danny was still staring as the elevator whisked Jake away to the fourth floor.

He had one last stop before press interview number three for the day. Lily's apartment. There were new people moving in—Lily's family, although Jake wasn't sure which family, exactly.

They had told Danny they didn't have much to move and wouldn't need help, but Jake was still going to at least welcome them to the Regency.

As the elevator door opened, he heard a man and a woman talking. The door to apartment 405 was ajar, and as he got closer, he could hear the couple debating the best place to put the television.

And a third voice, younger and slightly irritated, chimed in. "Just put it near the fireplace. I'm trying to enjoy all these cool pictures, and you're sending me bad vibes."

The voice sounded eerily familiar.

"Hello?" Jake said, knocking lightly on the doorjamb.

The girl was standing with her back to him, looking at the framed pictures Jake had laid out on the kitchen counter.

She turned around, and Jake gasped.

"Beth?" he said.

The girl looked at him like—and he'd seen this look before—he'd sprung antlers.

"Um, no. My name is Melissa."

"Melissa," Jake repeated.

"You okay, kid?"

Jake gave his head a shake. "You must be Lily's great-grand-daughter?"

"Great-great, I think. I'm never a hundred percent sure how that stuff works. Might even be another 'great' in there somewhere."

Jake nodded and held out his hand. "I'm Jake."

"I've heard about you, Jake. My parents"—she jerked her head toward the living room—"told me that Gram left this place to us. They say she liked you."

"I liked her. She was a sweetie."

"So . . . we're moving in." Melissa looked around at the faded paint and cracked plaster. "Not that I have a choice. Although the artwork is cool. I'm hanging these in my room. Should cover up some of the cracks."

"Yeah, about that. Be careful which walls you put nails into."

"I'm not a bonehead, Jake. I know about the murals. Gram left us instructions for how to take care of the apartment. A whole book."

Jake sighed happily. "Of course she did."

Melissa held up the framed angel. "She was talented. I know. I'm planning on going to art school someday."

"You'll have to see the work she did in the Great Hall."

"You the tour guide around here as well?"

"Sort of." His phone buzzed. A reporter from the local TV morning show. "I've got to take this. If you need anything, just let me know. I live upstairs, but there's a buzzer in the kitchen for emergencies."

"Sure. Thanks, Jake." Melissa went back to staring at the art.

He stepped into the hallway to take the call, but Melissa's voice drew him back.

"Jake?"

"Yup?"

"This place is a bit of a dump, isn't it?"

Jake smiled. "Definitely. But . . . we're working on it."

READER'S ACKNOWLEDGEMENTS

An acknowledgements section of a book is usually there so the author can thank people who helped make their book a real thing. But, and I'll explain this in my acknowledgements section, the author is only a part of the story.

So who do you want to thank for the opportunity to read this book?

AUTHOR'S ACKNOWLEDGEMENTS

You've probably noticed that there are two dedications and two sets of acknowledgements in this book. That's because this one, I think, comes closest to embodying my beliefs about books and stories.

I, as the author/illustrator of *Apartment 713*, am only part of what makes this book a story.

See, we get art wrong a lot in our world. We tend to think that an artist makes a thing—a sculpture, a painting, an object, a book—and that object IS the work of art.

The problem with this view is that we think the object is a finished thing. Especially when it comes to a book, this is one million percent false.

I've now written (and mostly illustrated) around thirty books, and my view has evolved. That's because my first novel, *Neil Flambé and the Marco Polo Murders*, is now more than ten years old. Tens of thousands of people have read that book. And each one of them has a *different book* in their heads and hearts.

Here's what I mean. I have written a story here (*Apartment 713*) that expresses what I want to say about a lot of things—architecture, friendship, the persistence of the past in our present, and more.

BUT there is no way that everything I feel, see, hear, think about the characters and this world can be written down on these few pages.

Which means that YOU fill in the rest. And we are not the same people. Jake and Beth sound different, look different, act different in your version of the book. You bring YOU to the story as much as I bring ME to the story.

So think of the book you've just read not as a finished product but as half of a circle. You fill in the other half, making it a richer, more vivid work of collaborative art.

And if you don't fill in that half, the book is less than nothing. It is just ink on a page.

But before I go, I do need to thank a few specific people.

I dedicated this book to Jack Kelly. After amazing dinners at his house (cooked by his amazing mom), Jack would take us on walks through Buffalo, New York. We saw some of the most amazing buildings and public spaces—designed by famous and creative people like Frederick Law Olmsted, Louise Blanchard Bethune, Louis Sullivan, Frank Lloyd Wright.

And we saw where beautiful buildings *used* to be, including a skyscraper designed by Frank Lloyd Wright. It was torn down before I was born, but I still feel the hole in the landscape where it should be.

That gave me a lifelong love for buildings that might not be cheap or quickly built, but that make the world a better place.

Of course, I must also thank:

My editors at HarperCollins: Yash Kesanakurthy, Suzanne Sutherland, Hadley Dyer, and Jennifer Lambert. Natalie Meditsky, Janice Weaver, and Lesley Fraser fixed up the words like expert masons. And Alan Jones did the same with the pics.

My friend Kenneth Oppel was a huge booster as I worked my way through this story. Thanks to Max and Gimli, the puppies, for snuggles and acting as sometime models.

All my family help all my work.

But huge props to my kid (and sometime co-writer) Basil, who helped me flesh out this idea.

My other kid Erin, for always keeping me filled with amazing baked goods. David helps too.

Laura, for everything.

And of course, thanks to you, the reader, for making this dead thing a live story.

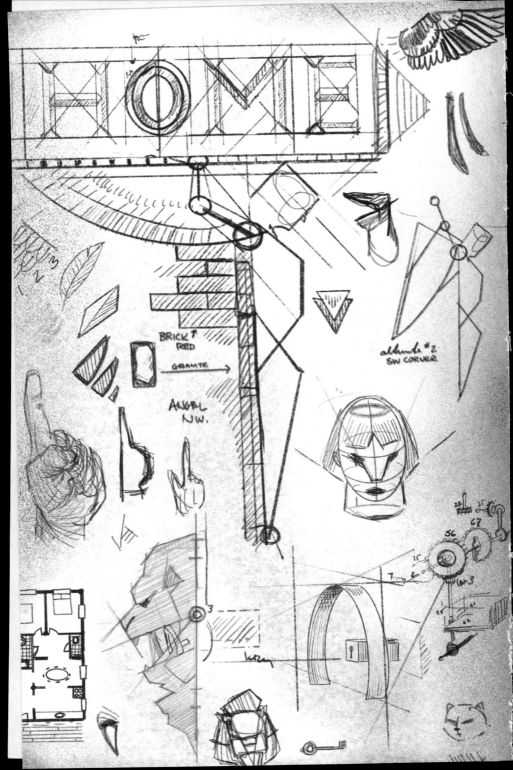